M000215758

THE RUNES OF VICTORY

THE SCEAPIG CHRONICLES BOOK 1

JOHN BROUGHTON

Copyright (C) 2021 John Broughton

Layout design and Copyright (C) 2021 by Next Chapter

Published 2021 by Next Chapter

Edited by Lorna Read

Cover art by CoverMint

Back cover texture by David M. Schrader, used under license
from Shutterstock.com

This book is a work of fiction. Names, characters, places, and incidents are the
product of the author's imagination or are used fictitiously. Any resemblance to
actual events, locales, or persons, living or dead, is purely coincidental.

All rights reserved. No part of this book may be reproduced or transmitted in
any form or by any means, electronic or mechanical, including photocopying,
recording, or by any information storage and retrieval system, without the
author's permission.

Imminet uero maximum insulae huic
et populo habitanti in ea periculum.
Ecce quod nunquam antea auditum
fuit, populus paganus solet uastare
piratico latrocinio littora nostra

An extract from a letter written by the scholar Alcuin from
the court of Charlemagne, addressed to the clergy and
nobles of Kent in 797 AD (See Appendix for translation)
Frontispiece by calligrapher Dawn Burgoyne

ACKNOWLEDGMENTS

I should like to acknowledge the encouragement and suggestions of my writer friend Randal Solomon (St Louis, Missouri) whose contribution has helped to make *The Runes of Victory* better.

Special thanks go to my dear friend and fellow writer, John Bentley, for his steadfast and indefatigable support. His content checking and suggestions have made an invaluable contribution to *The Runes of Victory*

EXPLANATORY NOTES

The pronunciation of some Saxon names might prove challenging to a modern readership. I hope this helps:

Sceapig = Sheppey
Cyneflaed = kinny-fled
Deormund = dee -or -mund
Saewynn = say - ee -wine
Eodred = ee-o – drid
Coelwulf = Seal – wolf
Cynebald = kinny – bald
Eadlac = Ed – lack

All other names should be read according to modern canons of pronunciation.

NB: originally the word viking was used to describe the activity of raiding and plundering.

Vikingr was the singular noun for the person who went viking. Vikingar was the plural noun.

ONE

SCEAPIG (ISLE OF SHEPPEY)

798 AD

DEORMUND TURNED THE WHITTLED OBJECT IN HIS HAND, not yet satisfied. Another trimming of the fipple, the mouth-piece of the horn whistle, a rigorous scraping of the flue and it was ready. The twenty-two-year-old never wasted a shed antler, carving them being an integral part of his life as a deer herder. The haft of the knife he'd just sheathed was his handi-work. He wondered how his best friend would respond to his latest piece of handcraft. Only one way to find out—he raised the whistle to his lips, blew, and it emitted a shrill note that carried on the sea breeze to the woodland where Mistig was passing the time.

He came, breaking out of the trees, bounding towards him, lolloping to a halt, his shaggy grey head tilted inquisitively as if to ask what adventure awaited. The deerhound's chest heaved, his tongue lolling after the exertion of his sprint to his master.

"It looks like the whistle will do, Mistig, if it brings you like that. You were so fast I should have named you Windig. But your name better suits your shaggy grey coat."

The hound wagged his tail, which was long enough to

1

touch the ground, the eager-to-please companion responding to the tone of his master's cheerful voice. Mistig was one of the main aspects of Deormund's life that made it so perfect.

He was the first and only deer herder on Sceapig—Sheep's Isle—all the other inhabitants being shepherds who bred, bought and sold ewes and mutton. The island was separated from the mainland of Kent by the Swale Channel, where ships sometimes sheltered from the fury of the open sea. This strait provided a natural barrier to predators, making life easier for those who tended their flocks or, in the unique case of Deormund, *herd*. His eye strayed to the southern side of the isle as he distractedly stroked the beard of his hound. That part of the island was marshy, crisscrossed by drains and inlets where the sun flashed off the sparkling water on this fine late-spring day. The silvery flashes, offsetting the white of the frolicking lambs and sedate ewes interspersed with the chestnut coats of his hinds, made him sigh. Was there a more perfect life? If there were, it probably pertained to a nobleman, he thought wistfully. Ay, those wealthy thegns who relied on him for their hunting ritual, not to mention, by association, the venison for their table.

"I'm glad I didn't follow in my father's footsteps to become a shepherd, Mistig. If I had, I'd never have brought you to Sceapig, would I?"

By way of reply, the seemingly fearsome, but docile, animal snuggled his flat head into his master's chest. He could do this because the deer herder was sitting on a smooth boulder, his favourite perch, likely deposited from the seabed by a storm. Folk could not imagine the appalling force of an enraged sea. The two remained locked in this amiable posture for some time, Deormund happy to reflect about his life on such a peaceful day and setting.

He sometimes wondered whether the choice of his trade had been determined unwittingly by his parents soon after his birth. When baptised a Christian, like them, in the church of the metal-workers' village across the channel, the priest of Faversham had asked, "What shall he go by?" and his father had replied "Deormund." It was not a common or even family name but, in accord with his parents, he liked it. *Mund means protection and the deor is a beautiful animal, especially the male* —Deormund identified with the stag, while his lean, muscular frame and chestnut-coloured hair and beard set many a *hind's* heart a-flutter on market days in Faversham! Not that Deormund had time for womankind, because his work as a *deer protector* absorbed him and rarely left him with idle time, such as these beatific moments of reflection. Besides, he considered himself too young to wed, which was nonsense, as his mother continually stated when nagging him to find a bride.

Was that his father down by the creek? He smiled fondly; it seemed to him that his father cared more for the ewes than the youngest of his three sons. At least he didn't badger Deormund about finding a maiden. He understood and approved of his son's dedication to his herd. But mostly, he appreciated the steady flow of coins that entered the family home, for Deormund unstintingly shared his hard-earned income with his parents. His elder brothers had chosen to gain a living in Kent. They kept a tight knot on their purse strings. In any case, Cynebald was a family man: his priorities lay justly with his wife and two girls. Cynebald's skill as a smith and reputation as a good husband and father was well-founded—he chuckled at his unintentional pun, causing Mistig's tail to wag again— "Well-founded, are you with me, boy? *Founded*, foundry, see?" He laughed heartily and the hound leapt away from his embrace and began to bound around, as much as to say, *haven't we work to do?*

They had, but Deormund was waiting for the wind. He needed to capture a new stag, preferably four years old or more.

It was the right time of year for trapping because the fierce stags shed their antlers this season, so capturing one would be less dangerous. The old boy that serviced the hinds was long in the tooth. Time for fresh blood. The wind was a problem; he had waited three whole days for it to strengthen. A stiff wind brought the deer out from the undergrowth to cruise along the downwind cover in untroubled search for feeding opportunities.

"You're right, my lad." Deormund addressed the hound, whose short ears were pricked to catch the nuances of his master's tone. Was this an allusion to work? There was nothing Mistig would prefer at that moment than a headlong chase after a stag. "We should take the ferry." The dog barked and wagged his tail in approval: he knew the word *ferry* meant work and exercise.

Deormund hurried home to collect his hunting bag and money pouch. The former contained a net to snare his prey, as well as twine and a rope for a leash. As soon as his mother, Bebbe, saw him swing the pack over his shoulder, she asked, "Are you off to Harty Ferry?"

Deormund sighed heavily, knowing that admission would lead to the usual request. "Ay, I'm away before the wind gets up."

Sure enough, the little woman, who was only tall enough to reach his breastbone, clutched his arm. "Wait, while I ready a package for our Eored."

She fussed around, wrapping cured sausages into linen cloth. She grasped a string net containing winter apples. "Here, put these in your bag. Eored should be fattened up; he was all skin and bones last time he came over. I don't know what you two have in your heads—un-carded wool, like as not! A man needs a good woman to look after him. Take our Cynebald, for example, he has two beautiful daughters!"

4

"Ay, that's all I need, another three women to nag me!"

He snatched up the proffered packages, stuffed them into his backpack and grinned provocatively at the tiny, loving woman, another lynchpin in his perfect life. Why should he swap her expert care and attention for a younger, inexpert version?

"I was going to stay with Cynebald, Wilgiva and the girls, but a visit to Oare will do just as well, I expect our wheelwright will be pleased to see his brother."

"Of course he will! Besides, Oare is only across the creek from Faversham; you can call in on your nieces easily enough."

She smiled fondly at her tousle-haired son, thinking proudly what a handsome catch he would make for some young woman. The object of maternal machination dodged through the door, accompanied by his impatient hound, overjoyed at the sight of his master's pack, a guarantee of adventure. As he hurried away, his mother's call to find himself a maid in Faversham was lost to his distant hearing.

The boatman, seated at the door of his hut, greeted them with a cheery wave as soon as they came in sight. Deormund and his hound were regular and valued customers, crossing the channel at least twice a month. Helmdag, the ferryman, liked the young deer herder who neither haggled nor failed to pay the fare, unlike many others. The boatman charged his passengers according to the weather conditions. Sometimes crossing the Swale set his toned muscles afire, other times the boat seemed to shoot across the three-hundred-yard stretch of water.

"You know a thing or two, lad!" The old ferryman tapped the side of his hooked nose. "Favourable current, backwind and no ebb plume from Conver Creek. I'll have you over there in a heartbeat!"

Deormund grinned, knowing it meant the fare would be lighter on his purse. The hound, used to ferry travel, was already sitting beside the rowing boat, his tail thumping the ground.

"Can you take me right into Oare Creek, Helmdag? I'm going to call in on our Eored."

"Right you are." the ferryman's strong pulls had sped them beyond midstream. "Is the young fellow still unwed?"

Deormund groaned inwardly. What was it with the people of Harty Island? Why could they not leave him and his brother happily unbetrothed?

"I hope so," he said, after a brooding silence designed to dissuade the boatman from further questioning. He had little success.

"You know how people will chatter?" the ferryman continued. Deormund nodded, he did know only too well. "I heard he's walking out with the miller's daughter. So, it'll be your turn next, young fellow-me-lad!"

With a stern expression, Deormund muttered an oath that was lost in the wind, which only served to earn him a broad grin. Much more of this and he'd threaten to become a hermit. Slipping a coin into the boatman's hand, he made his pleasant farewell, watching Helmdag pull strongly away from the wooden platform into the midstream of the creek. Mistig, already sniffing around this less usual landing place, re-established familiarity with a clump of heather.

"C'mon, Mistig, we're bound to catch Eored unawares!"

At the name 'Eored', the hound yapped and pranced around his master's feet, almost tripping him and eliciting a very unhuman growl that served to calm his exuberance.

Head bowed over his work, which consisted in repositioning a reinforcing panel on a cartwheel before nailing it into place, Eored saw only his brother's feet.

Without raising his head, he said, "Good afternoon, Deormund. What brings you to Oare?"

"Have you grown eyes under your hair? How did you know it was me?"

Eored straightened. "By your shoes—few people around here have footwear made of deer hide. Besides, I could see Mistig's huge grey paws next to you."

At the mention of his name, the hound began the ritual festivities, tail wagging, bounding around one of his favourite humans. As expected of him, at least by the dog, Eored ruffled his fur until the animal rolled onto his back to expose his stomach for stroking. Eored, who loved Mistig as if he was his own, obliged.

"So, what brings you to Oare?" he repeated.

"It appears that my mission is to fatten you up and check that you're betrothed."

The wheelwright tipped back his head, unwise in his squatting position over the hound, wobbled, and stood. "How is our mother?"

They chatted over such pleasantries until Eored suggested an ale in the nearby tavern. It proved to be a drink that would unexpectedly change the perspective of their sedate lives.

At the next table sat a man with a black eye and dried blood in his blond beard.

"Looks like he's been in a fight," opined Deormund idly.

"Frodwin? That's odd. He's a peaceable fellow, a sailor, he works out of Faversham for a trader in sheepskins and wine. They take the wool to Frankia and bring back wine. Let's cheer him by offering an ale. He must have a tale to explain the mystery."

A few casual remarks and they were soon engaged in conversation with the eager recipient of the ale.

"What happened to your face, friend?" Deormund asked.

As suddenly as a windswept cloud passes in front of the sun, the trader's countenance darkened.

"I'm in trouble now. Have to find another captain. I'll wager someone will want a man of my experience. He's dead, see?"

The brothers rightly assumed he was talking about his former employer. This, he confirmed. "They drowned poor Oswin in a barrel of red wine. Held his head under till his soul fled. That's how I got this swollen eye, trying to save him. I also got a lump on the back of my head that left me senseless. When I came to, there was no sign of our captain. They must have thrown him overboard. At least, they were carousing and half-drunk on the wine, likely their drunkenness helped me. They used my mates and me to roll the wine barrels over to the side and hoist them into their vessel. A beauty of a ship, theirs, long and narrow; I'd reckon twenty oars each side."

"Pirates then, but who were they?" Deormund asked exasperated.

Frodwin touched his bruised cheekbone gently but still winced: a gesture that the brothers separately thought reminded the sailor of his misadventure.

"They call themselves *vikingar,* which means sea-rovers in their language—another word for what you said, pirates!"

"Do you know whence they hail?" Eored asked.

"Where are they from? In my experience as a trader, I'd say they are from the far north, at the edge of the world. Take my advice, if you come across a vikingr, give him a wide berth. Those fiends are merciless—take what they did to Oswin because he tried to defend his goods."

"Yet, you live to tell the tale, friend."

The trader gave Deormund a sour look. "Ay, only thanks to the cask lid they'd prised off and flung into the sea. When we finished shifting the barrels, they had no further use for us and hurled all five into the sea. None of my mates can swim and they all drowned." His voice caught, causing him to pause to suppress his emotions.

The brothers waited respectfully as he took a long swig of ale. Setting down his beaker, he resumed his tale. "As I said, I was lucky. You can't stay afloat for long in these clothes, but I managed to reach the lid and cling on. I wager they were too drunk to notice, which accounts for why no arrow or spear struck. Saved by an act of scorn, for contempt was what it was when the vikingr flung the wooden cover into the sea. It buoyed me long enough for the current to bring me ashore. I reckon they must have boarded us a mile or so out of Herne Bay, where I washed up."

"In your misfortune, you were lucky, Frodwin. Another ale?"

"Ay, don't mind if I do. But mark my words," he stared hard with his unsettling injured eye, "if ever you come across the vikingar, expect no mercy."

That observation would return to haunt the brothers and shake them out of their perfect lives, miller's daughter and all.

TWO

NORTH KENT COASTAL AREA

798 AD

SAEWYNN, THE MILLER'S DAUGHTER, WHOSE PRETTY FACE, characterised by a liberally freckled turned-up nose and framed by flame-coloured hair, instantly endeared herself to Deormund. Following the rule, *love me, love my hound,* the deer herder beamed at the slim maiden who, upon encountering them as they left the tavern, ignored the two men in favour of Mistig by squatting and flinging her arms around the shaggy beast's neck, squeezing him to her breast.

Releasing her over-willing captive and looking up, she addressed Deormund. "What a lovely hound! What's its name?"

"I'm Deormund," he grinned, "and yon's Mistig."

The girl, realising her gaffe, flushed to the roots of her ginger hair. "Forgive me! You are Eored's brother, the deer man."

Deormund threw back his head and chortled; he wasn't about to spare her.

"Deer man? Well, I'm not about to sprout antlers if that's what you think!"

"Oh, come on!" Eored came to her rescue. "You know what Saewynn means." He smiled at his betrothed. "He's all right when you get to know him. It's just that—" he bit his tongue, leaving them both curious.

"What?" she asked

"Ay, just that ... *what?*" Deormund growled.

Eored racked his brains for a credible alternative. None came, so he completed his thought. "Just that he's not used to a maiden's company."

From the expression on Deormund's face, he knew he had blundered. Neither of them got another word out of the deer herder until they entered the wheelwright's small home. Not that it mattered, because Eored and Saewynn chattered all the way, absorbed in each other.

"Here, Mother sent you these. She thinks you need fattening up," he said, at last.

"Nay, my Eored's fine as he is. Besides, after our wedding," she gazed lovingly at her man, "I'll care for him well. We'll have no lack of freshly-ground flour for baking."

"So, when—"

"August. I've spoken to Father and the priest," she said quickly.

Deormund glared at his brother. "Don't you think you should go home and tell our parents?"

"We've only just decided. We've been together since before Yuletide—it's not been so long."

"Ay, well, why don't you two cross over the Swale with me when I take my new stag back?"

"You've still to capture it," Eored pointed out reasonably.

"I can sniff a change in the wind. I'll be hunting tomorrow and have you ever known us to fail?" He gestured to the hound stretched like a shaggy rug in front of the newly lit fire.

"Our Deormund knows his trade," Eored said.

"Is it hard to catch a stag, Deormund?" the young woman asked.

He studied the oval face and thought, *Eored's caught himself a lovely hind.* He appreciated the sincere interest in her eyes as she asked the question.

"Not if you tackle it correctly, Saewynn. That's why I mentioned the wind." He explained how he meant to set about it, casually throwing in the fact of the shed antlers.

"Ay, *those* would be a problem, I can see that. But what about when you've netted the beast? Doesn't it take some controlling?"

"It does," he eyed her figure, "it'll weigh about twice your weight, but when it realises I mean it no harm, and it's safely noosed, I shall lead it to the ferry. There are plenty of hinds on Sceapig to calm its nerves." He said this without considering his audience. Again, she flushed, making him feel clumsy and insensitive.

"Well, it's Nature," he said defensively, earning himself a sweet smile and confirming his positive impression of her.

The three ate a pleasant meal together until afterwards, Saewynn declared she had to go home. The brothers agreed to meet the next day at the ferry, at midday, with or without the woman, according to her father's ruling.

Deormund knew before rising that the wind had strengthened. He could hear it whistling around the roof of his brother's house. Devouring the crusty bread not finished the previous evening, he decided not to wake Eored since the dawn had not yet broken. No problem with Mistig, already sitting by the door, eager to bound outdoors. Deormund obliged, unlatching the door, settling his pack on his back before following the deerhound along the road towards the Forest Ridge. It was a long march, hence his early start. If he wanted to meet his brother at midday, he had to consider the time needed for the return.

Mistig bounded ahead, occasionally halting to check on his master and racing up to him only to lollop forward again, continually repeating the performance.

Dozy dog, you'll double the travel! Aware the hound revelled in exercise, he thought no more of it. After an hour of marching, the wind ruffling his hair and even snatching his breath away on occasions as it strengthened, he smiled to himself. *Perfect conditions for capturing a stag.*

He knew exactly where to place his net since this was the third time he had set out on a similar venture. Now the rising ground showed the forest on its ridge. That was his destination, just half a mile away. As he gazed up at the woodland, he imagined the activity therein at this time of day. Swineherds would be driving pigs along the main drove ways to the commons or dens. Deormund knew that in recent times, these clearings on the higher and better ground had become settlements. In the past, transhumance took place, the hogs could be many miles from the homestead; the changes made sense to him. Not that the villagers' activities particularly interested him.

Instead, he'd arrived at the area of concern to him: the fringes of this chalkland forest. He led Mistig to a track between two stately beech trees, ideal for hanging his net. Under the scrutiny of the intelligent hound, he removed it from his pack and spread it untangled on the grass. Taking his twine, he tied it just above head height around both trunks before tightly attaching his dangling net at its top corners. Next, he took two wooden pegs from the bag and pinned the lower edge into the earth. He used his weight to press each down with his foot, not hard enough to fix the net too firmly but so that any prey driving into the net would pull it free to complete the entrapment. Once the operation was ended, with the sagging belly of the mesh on the ground, all studiously watched by the hound, he headed several hundred yards farther up the edge of the forest with the wind behind him—an essential detail, because the buck could scent more than a hundred yards *upwind*. That was why he chose a place downwind at a fallen tree, so that he could sit on the trunk.

Judging that a couple of hours had elapsed since the dawn, he decided that soon a stag would break from cover to cruise with the wind along the woodland margin in search of food—if not, he'd send Mistig to chase one out. The hound, trained for months to do this, had succeeded twice before. Deormund had faith in his companion who, so giddy when not stalking but dedicated when at work, now lay with bearded chin on his crossed front paws, staring studiously along the line of the forest's edge. His master noted the gentle tremor running down the hound's body, a sure sign that the dog was like a coiled spring, suppressing his excitement.

Mistig suddenly bounded to his feet and was away faster than the wind. The deerhound had seen the stag before his master had even suspected its presence. Deormund leapt to his feet, snatched up his bag and shouldered it as he ran, never taking his eyes off the pursuit. Trained to perfection, Mistig only revealed himself some twenty yards from the net. At that point, he barked and accelerated, cutting off the startled and speedy stag, which, in terror at the sight of the snarling grey beast, swerved into the trees for cover, not suspecting the trap. When its charging hoofs took the deer into the trap, its head-long rush and weight pinged out the two pegs, ensnaring the struggling creature in the netting. The more it struggled to free itself, the more it became entangled. When Deormund arrived, out of breath, the beast was kicking and writhing in vain.

The deer herder, not forgetting his debt to Mistig, found a piece of his mother's sausage, preserved for the occasion, giving it to his worthy companion with words of gratitude and encouragement. Only then did he turn to inspect his flailing prize. It was a rusty red beauty: he reckoned, although the threshing about made it difficult to judge, that it stood about four feet, six inches tall. He would only be able to gauge its age by looking at its teeth; for the moment, he was happy to believe it was a five-year-old. This beast would have no trouble in ousting the old stag on Sceapig in the rutting season.

Ignoring the creature's panicked attempts to free itself, Deormund took his knife from its sheath and cut the twine attached to the beeches. Far from releasing the stag, this manoeuvre entrapped it further so that now it lay in the net on the ground, its eyes bulging and terrified. The deer herder prepared a rope noose, knotting it to slide and tighten easily, leaving a leash of eight feet. He did not wish to sustain a similar painful blow from the beast's hoof as on his first capture, which had left him limping for days and with a month-long bruise. Experience had taught him to be nimble and quick on his feet.

Now came the delicate part of the task: extrication. To do this, first, he took the loose end of the rope around the nearest beech trunk and tied it off, leaving the noose very large. Next, he knelt beside the animal and began to talk soothingly to it, making calm, reassuring noises as he freed the head and upper body from the netting, gently stroking the deer into stillness. The legs had to remain entangled until the last moment. As soon as he could, he slipped the noose over the beast's head and tightened it carefully around the neck. The time had come to free the limbs, which he did bit by bit, until the animal was cleared of netting. Released, the stag leapt to its hoofs and made to bolt, only to pull the noose tighter still around its neck. There it stood, captured, trembling and uselessly shaking its head.

Ready to dedicate time to his equipment, he rolled up the

net and packed it away, slinging his bag onto his back. Deormund then walked to the captive stag, where the creature shied away with the little slack the rope gave it. Gently, delicately, the deer herder stroked the velvety muzzle, soothing it again with murmured words. He noticed the nascent antlers, congratulating himself on an excellent morning's work. His hand slid along the cord until it came to the knot at the trunk. Knowing that it had been pulled tight by the stag, he grasped the rope with his left hand, hooking it under his armpit for extra security while sawing at the knot with his sharp knife. No point in trying to unknot the cord after it had been so tightened. At last, he was through it, sheathed his blade and seized the rope, now a leash, with his right hand.

For the moment, he would need all his strength. Right about that, he dug his heels into the ground as the stag bucked and tugged to escape. Steadily, Deormund hauled the creature towards him, stepping back out of the woods as he did so. Realising that there was no escape, the deer turned and, as the herder hoped, walked towards him. The stag lowered its head in a classic threatening gesture, readying for the attack.

"You'd better not do that when you've grown your antlers, my beauty!"

Mistig dashed over and, placing himself between the stag and his master, bared his fangs and growled ferociously as the captive rethought its strategy. Again, it turned to flee, but Deormund held firm and drew the would-be fugitive back out of the forest. The battle of wills lasted half an hour but ended in submission, as Deormund knew it would. By that time, they had travelled a mere eighty yards.

Thenceforward, it was a question only of leading the reluctant creature downhill. Judging by the sun appearing momentarily between scudding clouds, he had a good hour to reach the ferry.

"I TOLD you he'd do it!"

Deormund heard Eored's exulting cry from the jetty, as he rejoiced with Saewynn. She was overcome by the beauty of the stag and found the courage to approach to stroke its muzzle, much as the deer herder had done earlier. Passive and cowed, the creature submitted, much to her delight. Deormund was under no illusion: the hard part was yet to come—they would have to persuade the beast into the ferryboat.

"Over on yon pole, blow the horn, Eored, while I hold the deer still." He understood that the horn blast would not only advise Helmdag that they needed to cross the channel, but also terrify the startled stag.

The blast, after setting the animal bucking and kicking, brought a cheery wave from the boatman that Eored replicated. Once the boat had arrived, Deormund pulled the leash down the bank, but the terrified animal dug in its hoofs, stubbornly refusing to budge.

"Give me a hand, Eored. Nay! Not behind its rump if you value your clean breeches! Push its shoulder, that's right!" Between them, they succeeded in forcing the stag into the craft. Helmdag's strong rowing, aided by a stiff crosswind, transported the four humans and two animals across the Swale.

The stag did not show the same reluctance to leap out of the boat. Deormund almost lost his hold on the rope as he struggled one-handed to find his money pouch. Handing the cord to his brother, he settled the fare for everyone.

"We'll lead the deer—look, it's already feeding!—towards the rest of the herd and then let him loose."

They bade farewell to the satisfied boatman. It had proved a good day's work for him and the deer herder. As for Saewynn, she was anxious about meeting Bebbe, though convinced she could charm her husband, Asculf, the shepherd. She had likely underestimated how much Bebbe wanted her two younger sons to wed. Unbeknown to her, Saewynn would have an ally, not a jealous mother, to deal with, but she was right about Asculf.

Having approached his herd to a suitable distance, Deormund loosened the noose and allowed the stag to shake its head free. Oddly, the creature stood stock still for a moment, bemused. Raising its snout as if to sniff the air, it suddenly bounded at impressive speed towards the other deer. There would be no trouble between the two stags until the rutting season in September. Deormund did not doubt the outcome. They would both have ferocious-looking antlers by then.

Unknown to him as he considered this, and equally unknown to the loving couple, significant events would take place before the rutting season—one of them within a few days.

THREE

SCEAPIG (ISLE OF SHEPPEY)

798 AD

THE WORLD THAT DEORMUND CONSIDERED SO PERFECT was knocked awry after two blissful days. It is usually the way of things; just when everything appears unsurpassable, trouble befalls.

Those two days saw Saewynn accepted into the family, to Eored's unbounded joy, and the new stag's straightforward assimilation into the herd. The deer herder decided to delay his work to enjoy the presence of his brother and allowed himself to succumb to persuasion, accompanying the couple around Sceapig, visiting their favourite boyhood haunts and regaling the young woman with anecdotes from their youth. Amid much laughter and invigorating races on the meadow, they paused to study the rich fauna on the northern shore. Saewynn delighted in spotting an osprey and watched enchanted when it swooped to catch a fish in its talons.

"I'll wager you've never seen that before," she exulted, "admit it! I've brought you luck."

What sort of luck, they found out the next morning when trouble, in the form of Lord Octric, rapped on the door.

"Where is that layabout of a deer herder?" the thegn's son barked at the flustered Bebbe.

"I... I'll call him for you, Lord." She squeezed past the nobleman, noting his horse tethered to the fence and the presence of three other riders, who had dismounted and were holding their horses' reins.

"Ay, do that and be quick about it, slattern, or you'll feel the flat of my sword."

Eored, from his bedroom, had heard the abusive language directed at his mother, so it was all Saewynn could do to restrain him. But being lighter and no match for muscles acquired by hoisting cartwheels, he dragged her, still pleading with him, into the main room and thus, into the sight of the young nobleman.

"My, my, what have we here?" drawled Octric, gazing lustfully at the pretty miller's daughter. "What's a lovely creature like you doing in this hovel?"

Eored's rage, simmering, was about to explode, but luckily for him, his mother reappeared with Deormund in tow.

"Lord Octric! What brings you to our humble dwelling, without Thegn Sibert?"

"My father is on his sickbed." The nobleman modified his tone because, despite his arrogant bearing, he had respect for the deer herder, to whom he had come at his father's bidding for hunts two or three times a year since when he was a callow stripling. In those days, he had envied Deormund his strength and expertise and, above all, his free and easy life in the open air.

"I hope your father is not too ill," Deormund said, sincerely, because the thegn and he had an understanding. The nobleman had always maintained respect and his side of the bargain.

"Not too sick. The doctor says he overindulged at the table and should soon be back to his old self."

"I'm pleased to hear it. I expect you have come to arrange a hunt, Lord Octric."

"Ay."

"Well then, as with your father, you will choose a beast and I'll prepare it for tomorrow's sport. Shall we go?"

Deormund had not failed to notice his brother's angry expression and how he had pulled Saewynn to stand behind him, nor Octric's over-appreciative gaze when the woman retreated into the room, whence she had appeared. The deer herder needed no further reason to lead the thegn's son outdoors, across to his horse.

"I'll run on ahead, then you shall choose your game."

Deormund set off at a fast pace across the heathery turf, Mistig shooting past him. Physically, he was in good form, for his work required plenty of exercise. Even so, he could not maintain the sprint for more than three hundred yards and began to slow. He heard the drumming hoofs behind him but was not ready for the stinging blow across his buttocks. Halting to rub his burning flesh, he glared up at the rider who had delivered the blow with the flat of his blade.

Lord Octric leered down at him, laughing mockingly. "Why are you lagging? Do you think we have all day to waste, ceorl? Now, start running or you'll earn another taste of my steel."

Deormund had no choice, being an unarmed man against four warriors. As he ran as hard as his body would allow, he brooded that he might have fought the lordling had he been alone—scant consolation, this idle dream of what might have been. Back to the problem in hand, he halted. A running man and four cantering horses would disperse the herd all over the isle. Nobody wanted that, not even Octric, who wished to hunt on the morrow. Seeing him stop, the thegn's son drew nearer, unsheathing his sword, his intention clear.

Deormund spoke swiftly. "Lord, we must approach slowly on foot. You will recall how we always approach the creatures with your father."

Reluctantly, the lordling sheathed his weapon and leapt lightly to the ground, handing the reins to one of his retainers.

"Wait here, you three. The ceorl and I will proceed alone."

'Ceorl', is it? I could push him off a cliff and say he slipped!

For love and respect of Thegn Sibert, he knew that he would do no such thing; anyway, this part of the isle was devoid of cliffs.

"Steady, Lord," he reminded him. "We're upwind and can't get too close. When I come alone this afternoon to catch the beast you choose, I'll approach from yonder direction. You can see them from here well enough. Which one will it be?

"That one," Octric said without hesitation, pointing.

Deormund's heart sank. He could not sacrifice the new stag he had just captured with so much difficulty. His mind raced. Could he substitute it for the other, the older stag, on the morrow? Nay, the haughty swine would notice the switch. He tried persuasion.

"Nay, Lord, not good meat. You'd be well counselled to choose a tender hind for I have no doubt you will make the kill."

"Of course I'll make the kill, ceorl. Think yourself lucky you will not be my prey! A ceorl does not gainsay his lord."

"My lord's son. Your father never treated me in this way, Lord Octric."

"Do not bandy words with me, ceorl, or it will be the worse for you! I told you, I want that buck."

"But Lord, I strove so hard to capture it but three days ago. I plan to use him to improve the breeding stock."

"Since you are so clever, deer herder, you can go and ensnare another."

Deormund groaned, "Would that it were so easy! I beseech you, see there, that's a beautiful hind!" The young nobleman's eyes flashed and he grabbed Deormund by his arm, pushing his face to the deer herder's. Deormund shrank from the overpowering proximity as Octric began to speak.

"Listen well, there's only one *beautiful hind* that interests me on this damned island and it's the one back in your hovel. So, heed me well. It's either the deer or the girl—I'll have one or the other—and maybe both," he muttered, but Deormund heard him.

"Very well, you shall have the stag. Tomorrow, ride to the forest on the Ness." He pointed to the north-east where the promontory plunged in the sea.

"There you are, that wasn't so hard, was it? But I've half a mind to thrash you, anyway, ceorl!"

Again, the enraged visage thrust towards him.

A flash of grey and Mistig stood facing the lordling, growling aggressively.

"Go away, Mistig!" Deormund changed his voice to a scolding demand. "Go, I said!" he pointed towards home. The hound hung its head, tail between his legs, then, before Octric could react, bounded away to the building they had left earlier.

"Lucky again, ceorl; I'd have taken its head as swift as a blink." The nobleman pushed his blade back into his sheath.

Fool! Had I not stayed him, the hound would have ripped your worthless throat out!

He smiled at the thought, but should not have, because a bejewelled fist smashed into his face when he least expected it. A gem cut into Deormund's cheek, leaving him bloodied and procuring a scar later that would ever be a reminder of that day.

Deormund was not a violent man by nature, but his

stinging buttocks and aching cheekbone might require a measure of revenge. For the moment, he swallowed his pride and lied.

"Begging your pardon, Lord. I should never have contradicted you. It won't happen again."

"See that it doesn't, ceorl. Remember your father is a lowly shepherd, so your lands, flocks and herds and aye, even your womenfolk, are ours by rights!"

Deormund followed the nobleman a few paces behind back to the horses. He wiped his face with his sleeve. Shocked at the amount of blood staining the cloth, his resentment simmered.

"Be sure the stag is in the Ness Woods tomorrow—you know the price of failure," Octric leered, making a lewd, unequivocal gesture.

Deormund went to his boulder seat where he did his clearest thinking. His thoughts were in a tumult. First, he would not sacrifice his stag, but if he didn't, the lustful nobleman would seize and rape his brother's betrothed. He could not allow that. Nor could he warn Eored; his brother was the most hot-headed of the three. Octric and his bullies would have no compunction in slaying a rebellious ceorl. How could a good man like Thegn Sibert sire an arrogant brat like Octric?

Desperately, he hung his head, which was the moment he saw something that gave him an idea. The thegn was on his sickbed, therefore Octric would be in charge of the hunt. *Perhaps I can use the stag, after all,* he thought, as he bent to pick up the smooth, round stone, weathered and deposited there by the sea. If Octric behaved as he thought, he would want to slay the stag alone, to take the glory. Therefore, he would abandon his retinue to gallop ahead on the first sighting.

I know the lie of the land on the Ness better than anyone. It's full of sinuous gills connected by narrow 'shaws', the 'rewes', or what others would call thickets. Ay, there's just the place, though it will take careful planning. He turned the smooth, weighty stone in his hand, studying it attentively, then brought it to his lips to kiss before slipping it into his pocket.

All I'll say, back at the house, is that I'm setting up a hunt the same as ever. I won't mention any of this, not even to warn Eored to flee. I won't, because I'll make no mistake. Only I'll know about this; I can practise in the morning.

With that, he took out his antler whistle, gave it a blast and waited.

"You are a fine fellow. I know you would have done for the swine if he'd laid a hand on me—well, he did, but only after you'd gone," he said to the dog, whose head cocked to one side as its tongue lolled, "luckily for us both, old friend," he concluded, but then uttered, as an afterthought, "We'll sort Lord Octric out in the morn."

Mistig barked happily and, as Deormund rose from the boulder, bounded towards the house. *Look at him, without a care in the world! That's how I should appear to my family.*

It was impossible to maintain this resolution, because he walked into a heated exchange between Asculf, his father, and his brother. The shepherd had returned home from lambing, in high spirits, only to find his middle son tense and brooding.

"Ah, Deormund, thank goodness you're back, see if you can get some sense into your brother. He says Thegn Sibert's lad was eyeing his betrothed; she's with your mother at the moment. I've tried telling him, we can't stand up to the lords who rule over us."

"Well, I *can* and I will!"

"Keep calm, Eodred. Step outside a minute. I need to have a word with you—alone—" He cast a warning glance at his father, who shrugged and nodded.

When they returned indoors, Eored's face had cleared of thunder. "It's all right, Father, I'm sorry. I just lost my temper.

25

Lord Octric isn't like his father, but maybe he'll become a wiser man with age."

The shepherd bestowed his youngest son with an authentic look of respect. "Well, I don't know what you said to your brother, Deormund, but you've got him talking sense, at last. I began to despair. I did so!"

Deormund smiled and settled for silence.

If only you knew what I said, Father dear, you wouldn't be so content!

FOUR

SCEAPIG

798 AD

IT IS NO EASY MATTER TO KILL A HARE WITH A SLINGSHOT from twenty-five paces, a feat accomplished by Deormund several times since childhood. A superlative combination of skill and eyesight is needed to achieve the exploit. When he rummaged through his storage chest to retrieve the weapon, he had a larger game in mind. The beauty of a sling is that it is lightweight and easily hidden on the person. Another of the secrets of its successful use lies in the choice of missile. The deer herder had chanced upon the perfectly-shaped smooth stone the previous afternoon. It lay snugly in his pocket.

On his way to collect the stag, again by noosing it and leading with the leash, he would search for other similar stones to test that he had not lost his slinging ability.

Used to rising before the dawn, he did so once more, knowing that the arrogant lordling needed little excuse to chastise him.

He'll want his day's sport spread on a platter, Deormund thought bitterly, before snatching a crust of bread and a slice of mature sheep's cheese. He ate on the move as he hurried by a

27

circuitous route to the meadow, thus ensuring that he was downwind from the herd. In his right hand, he carried a coil of rope that ended in a wide loop; casting the noose was another of his talents, essential to his trade. The herder had perfected this technique because the management of the herd called for two-yearly culling. If he did not capture the beasts, there could be no cautious thinning of the population. No lynxes, bears or wolves inhabited the island, so Deormund took their place as the predator, but only for selective slaughtering.

The early morning sun spread a comforting glow across the estuary. The deer were already grazing; their feeding ensured no chance of long grass or tall shrubs on the meadow. For this reason, walking was easy and silent underfoot, allowing the deer stalker to steal unnoticed towards the herd. To his satisfaction, the stag he sought grazed among the nearest hinds to his approach, so, at the last moment, he grasped the noose, widening it before sprinting forward. Simultaneously, he spun the rope around above his head, gaining momentum until, with precision, he released it to sail over the head of the alarmed and fleeing animal. In seconds, the cord pulled tight around its neck. Almost as if resigned to a familiar fate, the stag skidded to a halt. Its grazing companions had all fled to remain at a hundred yards' distance, staring back as if anxious about the fate of their consort.

Deormund understood them and his captive, to whom he spoke soothingly as before, leading the animal easily this time, away from the herd and towards the Ness Forest.

"Don't worry," he told the stag, as if whispering confidentially to a friend, "I will not let them hurt you."

From a young age, his father had permitted Deormund to explore the forest, without fear of wild beasts, and Asculf worried only about the unexpected rills and treacherous declivities. For that reason, he pointed out all the dangers to his sons.

Not a single corner of the woodland remained unknown to the youngest. Therefore, whilst sitting on the boulder the previous evening, Deormund had decided where to place the stag. Touching the stone in his tunic, he considered that if fortune smiled upon him, he might not even be the direct cause of the lordling's demise. The forest boasted a particularly dangerous gorge, where one could arrive at a gallop without the horse sensing the danger: the ideal place to lure his victim.

Deormund's plan was diabolical and premeditated; nonetheless, he had scruples. Only the threat of choosing to sacrifice the hard-gained stag or Saewynn's virtue, drove him to set the trap. His liking for the scoundrel's father, Thegn Sibert, caused him further pain, but frankly, he saw no choice. If Octric did not plunge headlong into the gorge, he would be ready with his sling.

I'm not a coward: I sought this not. Besides, if I'm discovered by his followers, I'm a dead man!

These were his thoughts as he led the stag around the farthest edge, to the opposite side of the narrow ravine where an abundance of undergrowth sheltered him from the onrushing pursuers. He looked into the large, brown eyes of the gentle creature.

I hope to God, I'm right about this, otherwise you'll finish up dead meat first, my friend.

Embracing the stag around its neck, he slid off the noose, but for his plan to work, he had to hobble the animal, so he transferred his grip to the hind leg where, with a deft manoeuvre, he slipped the noose around the limb and pulled it tight. The other end of the rope, he tied around a sturdy trunk. Before settling into a hide whence he could keep an eye on the opposite side of the gorge, he led Mistig back around to the trail on the other side.

"Go! Fetch the riders!" The expert hound, used to many

previous deer hunts, understood its duty and bounded away. Deormund, who did not doubt Mistig's abilities, hastened back to the shelter he had chosen: a hawthorn bush. Dispassionately, he watched the stag kick at its tether, but soon lose interest in favour of the tempting grey lichen growing on a fallen trunk. With grim satisfaction, he noted that the rope, hidden by the tall undergrowth as planned, could not be seen from the opposite side of the chasm. An approaching rider would see only the head and shoulders of the beast.

When it came to hunting, Octric and his friends were disposed to rise early, so to Deormund's relief, he soon heard the distant thumping of hoofs. Mistig appeared first and, as trained, stood pointing his snout in the direction of the quarry. A deerhound must not frighten away the game when hunting.

The sound of drumming hoofs drew nearer, matched by Deormund's accelerating heartbeat. According to plan, the deer herder spotted Octric galloping headlong through the trees. The rider saw the hound, knew the significance of its frozen pose, his eyes following to settle on the stag, so, spurring on his mount, he nocked an arrow. Deormund readied his stone in the sling whilst admiring Octric's horsemanship. It was no easy matter to hold on to a galloping horse with the knees and, at the same time, wield a bow and arrow. As he had hoped and planned, he did not need the sling. Octric's steed, realising the peril, at the last second hunched its shoulders to dig its forelegs into the ground, pitching its unsuspecting rider over its head into the rocky gorge. Quickly, aware of thundering approaching hoofbeats, Deormund hacked through the rope, releasing the stag to bound away, still trailing the cord. If caught, the deer herder knew he would be in serious trouble, but he hoped that the plight of their master would put an end to the hunting.

Mistig had run to the edge of the chasm to stand there, barking frantically. Deormund could not allow himself to be seen, so he remained concealed, contenting himself with envying the hound's vantage point. Could anyone survive the fall? He fervently hoped not, even if, for the moment, no blame could be attached to him. Nay, he would stay well-hidden and hope that the deerhound would not betray his presence—that would be a disaster!

Alerted by the hound and the riderless steed, the Octric retainers reined in. The oldest among them, quick to understand, bellowed orders; Deormund recognised a Dorset accent.

"The horse has thrown Lord Octric into the chine! You two, climb down, careful now! See if he needs aid."

The chosen men dismounted, peered over the edge and started the treacherous descent. At the bottom of the ravine, a stream ran through rocks where the battered body lay motionless. Deormund did not know what they would find, although he suspected. Their voices drifted up indistinctly, so it wasn't until many minutes later, when they had climbed laboriously back up the side, their curses ringing out as footholds proved unreliable, that he heard: "There's nought for it. Lord Octric's gone; his skull is smashed. God rest his soul!"

"We must bring up the body. His father will want a Christian burial," the leader said.

Deormund took the stone from his pocket, laying it on the ground, for now he would not need it.

I don't have his blood on my hands!

He stopped his conscience-stricken reverie when he heard his name mentioned.

"We'll need rope to recover the body. The deer herder will have it. Let's ride back. Master Deormund will know what to do."

To the deer herder's relief, they turned their horses and rode away. His relaxation was greater still when he saw Mistig bound after them. He was safe. But how could he get back home before them?

Gazing thoughtfully at his chosen stone, he picked it up again and slipped it back in his pocket. Even taking a shortcut, he could not match the speed of their horses. Eored would have to provide the rope they required in his stead. He would go down to the meadow as if nothing had happened; there was always work there.

The question of the stag trailing a cord troubled him, but he doubted that the beast would find its way to the pasture with people around. It would remain under cover, feeding content-edly. Deormund smiled grimly. Saewynn's virtue was intact and no longer endangered.

If he hadn't died, he'd have eaten my stag and taken my brother's wife, too. I'm sure of it. God forgive me, but he had it coming.

Before the deer herder left the woodland cover, he found a small glade, where he knelt, bowed his head and prayed.

Lord, I cannot confess my sin to any man, but I beg your forgiveness, for You are a just God and Protector of the weak. Help me repair my sin by aiding others in need. He paused, lost for words, never having found prayer easy, then ended lamely, *Forgive me, Father, for I have sinned. Amen.*

From the glade, a narrow trail led down the side of the promontory to the shore. Changing his mind about the meadow, with the tide low, he could walk along the shore. There might be some cockles for his mother's pot and they would provide a convincing excuse as to his whereabouts during the tragedy. There was a place about five hundred yards ahead where he was sure to find a plentiful supply. Taking off his shoes, he waded into the shallow water and let a wave refresh his tired legs before twisting his toes into the sandy bed. Soon, he had brought several cockles to the surface, which he picked up, throwing back a small one, keeping the large, which he thrust into his tunic with the slingshot and stone. Before long, his pocket was bulging, so he recovered his shoes and laced the thongs around his ankles before setting off with a cheery whistling towards home.

His eye roved over the waves. What was that in the distance? A ship with a square sail emblazoned with what? There was an emblem. He squinted against the strong light. The billowing cloth depicted a black bird with outstretched wings—a raven maybe. Not understanding the significance of what he had just observed, he put it out of his mind; after all, there was a stag somewhere trailing a rope—the only tangible proof of his guilt. First, he would take the cockles home, play the innocent, then maybe get Mistig to help him round up the elusive deer. Octric's men would be too busy recovering the body and taking it back to Faversham to catch him covering his crime—if, indeed, 'crime' was what it should be considered.

Crossing the meadow, he came upon Mistig, bounding towards him as if he'd been away for a month. He bent to stroke the fussy hound, but their reunion was abruptly interrupted.

"Oi, Master Deormund! Come quickly, you're needed!"

The Dorset accent identified the rider.

"What's wrong? Did you miss the stag?"

"Ay, we did. But the worst of it is we lost Lord Octric."

"Lost him? What, has he gone astray in the forest?" The convincing tone and surprised expression came naturally and deceived the retainer.

"Nay, I would it were so! He rode ahead of us all and plunged into a chine."

"Is he...is he—?"

"Ay, dead! It is a great misfortune, Master Deormund. With our lord still recovering his health, an' all—this will set him back."

"If he's dead, why do you need me?"

"We must recover the body. We'll need ropes. I asked your brother but he says you'll know where they are."

"How hard is it to find my ropes?" Deormund grumbled. "Let's go. I have cockles for mother's pot."

"Ah, so that's where you were."

Deormund smiled inwardly, hastening towards the house, only vaguely worried about the rope-trailing stag.

Deormund rode out with Octric's men on their master's horse. The deer herder pretended he didn't know which part of the forest the body lay in but insisted on a description of the place.

"Ah, I know the likely spot," he said convincingly, "it's dangerous, right enough," and led them there.

They recovered the body using a litter and ropes. The difficulty of the recovery underlined the danger he'd mentioned.

"Lord Octric must have spotted the stag across the gorge," Deormund said ingenuously. "His horse will have stopped just as he was aiming, I'll wager."

"That's how it happened, for sure," the Dorset man concurred. "What ill luck! Hoist the body over his mount and we'll get back to Faversham to break the sad news."

"I'm deeply sorry," Deormund lied. He followed the slow procession back to the meadow whilst Mistig ran ahead. Only when they headed towards the ferry, did he turn around to go home to deposit his ropes and think about what had happened.

The stag will keep till the morning.

That was his only concern, never imagining that more serious matters lurked on the horizon.

FIVE
SCEAPIG (ISLE OF SHEPPEY)
798 AD

THE PEACEABLE FOLKS OF SCEAPIG, IF ASKED IN 798, would have shrugged and denied all knowledge of people calling themselves *Vikingar*. The new century was about to change that, when everybody would live in terror of *The Northmen* and call them Vikings. They embarked on Sceapig for the first time in the late spring of 798, a disaster for Deormund because it was calving season for many of his hinds.

Unlike his family, fortuitously, he was absent when the longship crew came to his home. The deer herder was in the Ness Forest with Mistig, attempting to track and recapture the stag to reintegrate it into the herd. In the depths of woodland, a man is lost to the outside world and its goings-on. Deormund spent all morning hunting the wily beast but at last Mistig trapped it in a small clearing, enclosed on two sides by a sheer rock face some ten feet high—a small cliff the intimidated creature could not scale to escape. Mistig's warning bark—to fetch his master, not terrify the stag—still had that effect, so that the entrapped stag risked all, to plunge past the hound.

Taken by surprise, his work undone, the deerhound had the

presence of mind to seize the trailing rope between its teeth to cling on, despite being dragged along the ground. How the dog would have fared, Deormund could only guess, because he arrived in time to grasp the rope and join the growling hound in pulling back on the rope. The hobbled creature had to surrender or break a leg. Luckily, it gave in so that the deer herder transferred the noose back around the stag's neck. The chase over, and after rewarding Mistig with a treat from his pocket, the time had come to return through the forest towards the meadow.

There, a shocking sight met the herder's eyes. A dozen men, some of them with wolf pelts over their shoulders, were slaughtering his father's sheep and his deer with spears. Their aim was not always true, especially with the deer whose swiftness saved many but, sorrowfully, he watched several pregnant hinds scream, wounded, or killed because they were less nimble. His heart bled for them while a red mist descended over his eyes. Who were these fiends? He still had not associated them or their longship with the words of the trader in the tavern. Whilst he hesitated at the forest edge with his leashed stag, one of the marauders pointed to him so that their leader ran, brandishing a sword and calling in a strange, incomprehensible tongue.

Deormund turned and sprinted back in among the trees, confident that none of the intruders knew the woods as well as he. Making for a small clearing, he heard the chieftain's crashing footsteps in pursuit. Halting in the centre of a glade, there was just time to tether the stag and draw the slingshot from his pocket. He placed the stone intended for Octric in the sling and swung it around his head, thinking of his mother's tale of King David and the giant Goliath.

The huge, blond-haired invader burst into the clearing brandishing his sword; like the Biblical giant, he had no time to react; the stone hit his forehead so hard that he crashed dead to the ground. Deormund raced over, retrieved the missile, pocketed it and the slingshot, hesitated, then unbuckled the belt with a sheath, picked up the fallen sword and made them his own. Snatching up the large, round shield, he took that, too. Hearing more noisy steps approaching, he dashed to the stag, used the sharp blade with relish to slice the restraining cord and, with the two animals, darted along another trail. As they fled, he distinctly heard enraged, guttural voices. The pursuing band came after him, but they would not catch him; he would lead them to where Octric had met his doom. To effect this plan, he needed to run faster so that he could circumvent the ravine.

Just in time, he reached the opposite side of the gorge, where he stood until he saw them sprinting towards him with raucous war cries. He trembled, but raised and brandished the sword, taunting the onrushing warriors. With him firmly in their sights and vengeance for their leader on their minds, they did not look underfoot. The first two fell screaming into the gorge. The next two halted but the men behind, running in headlong fury, crashed into them, sending them teetering over the edge to their deaths.

From Deormund's throat burst forth a victory howl; he pulled the stag and, with Mistig, set off at speed once more as a spear flashed past his hip to bury its point in the ground. No others arrived, for the Vikings lost time checking on their dead and trying to find a way around the gorge.

Meanwhile, the deer hunter and his prize stag sped away to a secret place even his brothers did not know, a concealed cavern, where he could hide until the next day if necessary. The deer and dog would have to come inside, out of sight, too, because sheer misfortune might bring the enemy into proximity, although he doubted it.

Inside the cave, he had the problem of how to tether the stag. This occupied his thoughts for a few minutes; he even considered tying the rope around his own ankle until he saw it. A tree root had grown through the friable rock and, as roots do, had thickened over the years. It disappeared into the cave floor; not even a healthy stag could snap a tap root. Securing the cord, he turned his attention to Mistig, instructing the hound to be still. The dog, having had the word *still* drummed into him since he was a puppy, laid down at his master's feet and pretended to be dead.

Time stood still inside the refuge. The deer herder whiled away the time thinking. Reflecting on what had happened and studying the sword and shield, he convinced himself that these intruders were the infamous Vikingar of the tavern conversation. Sadly, he realised that the perfect island home he so loved was no longer so ideal. Exposed to the raiders' ships, this peaceful paradise was vulnerable. Determined not to be a passive victim, he would learn to fight. After all, how many ceorls could afford a sword like the one he possessed? None. The decision was taken: the next day, or whenever the pirates had gone, he would take his first steps in learning a new occupation—that of the warrior. How to go about it was clear to him.

Next, he considered his present trade. It had suffered a severe blow. At least six pregnant hinds, their eight month's gestation almost up, had been slaughtered before his unbelieving eyes. Curse the Vikingar! Thankfully, he had saved his precious stag; first, from a foe of his race and then, from the hitherto unsuspected strangers. If they came back, he swore he would be ready for them. Perhaps they would never reappear, but on that score, he had a presentiment. In any case, the breeding season would come around again in a few months. The sturdy creature that was with him in the cavern, so far had brought only bad luck, but it would repair the damage sustained today.

Suddenly, Deormund leapt to his feet, startling Mistig and the stag. His hunter's instinct told him that the Vikingar would have abandoned their pursuit, however enraged they were with him.

I reckon I killed at least five, one way or another he consoled himself. *They paid a high price for my hinds and Father's sheep. Oh, my God!* He had not thought about his parents' safety. Maybe they had met the same fate as their animals. He had to find out. Again, he felt the perfect balance of the Vikingr sword and admired its honed edge as he severed the rope from the root.

Deciding to take a circuitous route to the fringes of the forest for safety's sake, he approached the edge on the leeward side of the Ness, where, before breaking cover, he tethered the stag. Dropping onto his stomach, he wormed his way to the break in the trees and peered out, down to the shore. There before him lay an incredible tapestry. Drawn up on the beach was a longship, its sails furled, whilst on the sand there were three fires with groups of men clustered around, roasting the stolen meat on spits. Deormund ground his teeth at the thought of *his* hinds being consumed by pirates. Still, consolation was not tardy in recompensing him because, accompanied by a mournful lament, four men carried a body to a pyre of driftwood and forest branches piled into a small boat. They dragged the vessel into the sea. No doubt it was the chieftain slain by his trusty sling; he touched the smooth stone in his pocket and smiled grimly as the foe threw a torch into the piled tinder in the craft under the body. He only wished the wind would sweep the blazing, drifting boat into the mother ship, but that did not happen. The flames lit up the twilight and reflected in the waves. The lament died away, to be replaced by ringing cheers and brandished axes and swords. It seemed the Vikingar, in some way, were pleased for their departed lord. Years later, Deormund would learn about Valhalla, but for the moment, he was confused in his ignorance at their revelling and lack of seemliness. Raucous feasting at a funeral shocked him.

He deemed it safe enough to return to his home. Were his parents, Eored and Saewynn unharmed? He needed to know. He decided to take the stag with him to the house, where he would place it in a small enclosure built years ago, rather than risk losing it to the troublesome invaders. Would they leave at night? He doubted it; more likely at dawn. Now, they would feast and drink, maybe to celebrate a new chieftain— he could only guess, knowing nothing much about their customs.

When he approached his home, wary of Vikingar lookouts but seeing none, the sight of smoke curling above the roof reassured him. Someone had lit a fire.

There's no smoke without life! Running to the door, he burst in to come face to face with his father holding a pitchfork threateningly. Had he arrived faster, he'd have impaled himself on the prongs!

"Deormund! We feared you were slain!"

"I, too, feared for you, Father! But what of Eored?"

"He saw them coming and fled to the ferry with Saewynn. I hope they got across the channel. He wanted to warn Thegn Sibert. Eored said the thegn could raise the fyrd. They came here, you know. They wanted meat. I offered them our salted meat. They spat it out and struck me twice, but I reckon they thought Mother and I were no sport because of our age; they laughed, made sheep noises and deer roars, spat at us again and left."

"Ay, they slaughtered your ewes and my hinds. The swine are feasting on them even now."

"But you, Deormund? How did you escape their wrath?"

"I slew some of them. Five, I think."

He recounted the tale of his adventures. His father took him in an embrace. "I'm proud of you, my son, but I fear you are in danger."

"We all are, Father. I suspect they will wish to avenge their chieftain—the one I killed first. I hope that they will sail away at dawn. They may be dismayed by their leader's death and not yet ready to trust a new one, but for sure, sooner or later, they will return."

Luckily for young Deormund, although his prediction was correct, the timing was to his advantage—although, at that moment, he could not foretell that his father would not live to see the Vikings again.

The next morning, before dawn, Deormund left Mistig and the sword with his father, took his slingshot, stone and the newly acquired shield and crept across the meadow to spy on the Vikings. His timing was perfect because, as he lay behind some clumps of heather and peered down on the shore, he saw the raiders push their beached ship into the sea and clamber aboard. Oars dipped and flashed in the early morning half-light so that soon, the vessel had turned about and, as the large sail dropped down, it filled with wind, sending the longship scudding on the ebb tide out into the open sea.

Good riddance! Deormund's heart sang. When he judged they were far enough away to no longer see a figure on land, he stood, shook a fist at them, cursed them to Hell, and waited long enough to assure himself they had no intention of returning. Only then did he run back home to retrieve the stag and reintroduce it into the herd. As soon as it was released, the creature bounded to join the other animals and, for the first time in days, Deormund felt relief course through his body. Foreboding at the Vikingar return prevented him from exulting, but at least there was hope that this had been but a fleeting troublesome period. His wise young head told him not to be overconfident, but to proceed with his plan. Doing so would reassure him that Eodred and his betrothed were safe, apart from allowing him to press ahead with his scheme.

So, he went home to tell his parents that he was about to take the ferry and was unsure when he would return. His father promised to keep an eye on the deer, although, aside from freak weather, there was little for him to do. One or two hinds might need assistance with birthing, but the shepherd was used to helping the ewes. Deormund left Mistig with his father and set off to greet the boatman.

SIX

FAVERSHAM, KENT

798 AD

THEGN SIBERT CHOSE NOT TO MEET DEORMUND AT ONCE; instead, he spoke privately with his Dorset warrior—a man who had gained his trust. "Bring his sword to me and organise the rest."

The veteran hurried to do his master's bidding, explaining the situation to the confused deer herder. "You are to leave your weapon for the thegn to inspect. Unbuckle it!"

Despite his bafflement, Deormund obeyed and, since his head was bowed over his belt, he barely noticed the warrior indicate a servant to fetch a staff from a stave rack.

"Here, take this staff. A man should not wander the streets unarmed."

Deormund exchanged the sword for the wooden pole—a poor affair, he thought, but, unused to the ways of the mainland folk, he did not dwell on the matter.

"Come back at midday. Thegn Sibert will receive you then and return your blade."

Outdoors, wandering the streets of Faversham distractedly, lost in thought about his strange reception, Deormund walked

43

straight into a trap. In truth, a sturdy fellow with a staff in hand barged into *him*, crashing into his shoulder.

"Hey!" cried the startled deer herder.

"Watch where you're going, clumsy oaf!"

Hurt and offended by the insult, Deormund raised his stave for combat. That was all the other man wanted, not hesitating but aiming his staff violently at his adversary's head. The deer herder instinctively warded off the blow but it was so forceful that his arms juddered, while his assailant grinned cockily. Deormund hadn't wielded a staff since his youth when he fought his brothers regularly in mock combat. Still, his past training served to prevent the other from breaking his bones. Rather, the problem he experienced, an inability to hit his opponent, handicapped him. The uneven contest dragged on with Deormund on the defensive, until a third party with a staff arrived and a fourth.

"Lend a hand with this stranger, Ingulf!" his foe cried.

Deormund, from the corner of his eye, saw the strike coming and nimbly jumped aside, at the same time sweeping his stave around to crack the newcomer on his kneecap. The man howled with pain, but his associate rushed in whilst the outnumbered islander parried a mighty blow from his original attacker. The fourth man, behind him, sent him staggering with a painful strike to his back. Although one of his attackers was hobbling and severely incapacitated, Deormund sensed that he was in serious trouble. Something unexpected needed to happen to save him.

Help came in canine form. Mistig had gone off to explore his surroundings when his master had not allowed him to enter the thegn's hall. Hound and owner had forgotten about each other for a while; yet, when the deerhound rounded a corner, he smelt his master's fear and, seeing him in a fight, the dog transformed into a grey-furred missile. Flinging himself at the assailant's back, he knocked him off-balance, enough for Deormund to deliver a resounding crack on the fellow's skull. The man pitched senseless to the ground with Mistig standing growling over him, whilst turning an evil eye onto the limping man with a staff, hesitating over whether to abandon what was becoming an ill-fated encounter.

"Enough, Ingulf! Leave him be! They didn't tell us he had a bloody great hound."

"Come on, Mistig," the deer herder called, then laughed and said, "Let's find a friendlier welcome elsewhere!" He shouldered his stave and strolled away, whistling nonchalantly for the benefit of the scoundrels bending over their unconscious comrade.

He found a waterside tavern where he bought a jug of ale and haggled over the price of a beef bone for Mistig. The silver coin agreed upon was well spent, if expensive; after all, the hound had turned the contest in his favour. He raised the beaker to his lips, noticing that his hand trembled, likely from the tension brought on by fighting.

"Welcome to Faversham!" Deormund said bitterly, his tone causing Mistig to cease his gnawing and look up at his master. "I'm all right, old fellow, thanks to you!" he said gently, patting the dog on its head and receiving a cautionary growl for bringing his hand too near to the juicy bone; nonetheless, the hound's tail thumped amicably on the reed-strewn floor.

Pouring another measure from the jug, Deormund thought about what had occurred. Shrewd as ever, he considered that the circumstances of the altercation were curious. First, why pick a fight with a stranger over a simple jostle? The fellow had been spoiling for a fight, but why? Second, it was no coincidence that two other men with staves happened to be passing by. He had subsequently walked from the skirmish to this tavern without seeing a single person carrying a staff, among all those he'd passed on the road. Third, why had the Dorset man warned him to take along a stave?

"Nay, there's more to this than meets the eye, boy," he addressed the hound, which, by way of reply, crunched the bone with his back teeth and swept the floor with his tail.

"It must be near midday; we'd better be going."

The deerhound leapt up, reluctantly hesitating over the bone, but Deormund raised a warning finger in front of the hound's face, picked up the treat and thrust it into his back-pack. The dog, understanding, wagged his tail and bounded to the tavern door, turning to gaze expectantly at Deormund.

His hand lingering over the latch, he told his faithful companion, "Stay by me!" He was concerned about meeting more villains with staves or cudgels. Mistig understood the command, often used when stalking, so walked beside his master, keeping apace up to the thegn's hall. By the outside wall of the building, Deormund unlaced his pack, took out the bone and tossed it to the hound. "Wait here!"

A surprise awaited him indoors. Thegn Sibert, the Dorset warrior and the three earlier assailants stood together, relaxed and talking.

"Ah, Deormund! Welcome to my home. You will forgive me if I have put you to the test. You have met Wardric." He pointed to the ruddy-faced veteran from Dorset. "He tells me you slew the Vikingar and took his sword. It is a fine weapon. Here, take it. I wanted you to prove your mettle as a fighter to be sure that you killed the Northman. It's easy enough to unbuckle a sword from a man who has died in an accident. But my men tell me that you are a worthy opponent. Just look at the lump on Ingulf's brow!"

The fellow in question glared at Deormund and was about to say something, but thought better of it and held his tongue.

The thegn grinned and raised an eyebrow. "So what is it you want of me, deer herder?"

"Lord, these Vikingar are fiends. They came unsuspected to Sceapig, slew my hinds in calf and threatened my parents. I fear that this was not a one-off attack."

The thegn, recognising that he was not dealing with a simple ceorl, gazed astutely at the islander. "Deormund, I have had dealings with you over the years and always found you an honest and well-organised hunt-planner. I repeat my question —what is it you want of me?"

"Forgive me, Lord. I have a sword. I killed their chieftain and maybe four others, but by cunning, not combat. I know not how to wield this weapon. Yet, I know these pirates, fearsome as they are, can be beaten. I wish to learn to fight and join with you to resist them when they return."

The nobleman stared at Deormund for a long, uncomfortable moment in which the deer herder wondered if he had overstepped a mark. The thegn sighed heavily. "Would that it were so simple, Deormund. You are a good man; I can use one like you. You have my word; I will have Wardric train you to fight with a sword. But there is much you do not know about the pirates. Tomorrow, you will travel with my party to visit the Archdeacon of Christ Church, Canterbury. Soon, you will know more about them than is good for your peace of mind. Now, you will eat with me and befriend your foes of earlier!"

Over the meal, the thegn explained that the archdeacon had summoned many landowners to Canterbury for a meeting about the Northmen. Deormund was surprised to find that the problem of the marauding *Vikings*, as Thegn Sibert called them, went well beyond the confines of the island of Sceapig.

So, the next day, the deer herder, who had not travelled farther afield than Faversham, its surrounding villages and woodland, took the road to Canterbury. On arrival, to his eyes, the city seemed overcrowded. There was a large market whose stalls appeared to stretch in an endless line, with wares and colourful spices he had never seen before or even imagined. As for the number of churches, taverns, shops and workshops, it left him so impressed that he would have sworn readily that Canterbury was the biggest city in the world.

Thegn Sibert led them to a large building with an ornately carved doorframe. On closer inspection, the carvings were of angels and saints worshipping a babe in a manger.

"The archbishop's palace," the thegn said, noting Deormund's wide-eyed examination of the decoration.

"Fit for a prince," the islander murmured.

"Ay, Wulfred is a prince of the Church."

That explains it then—Archdeacon Wulfred is a prince.

Such was Deormund's not altogether ingenuous reaction.

"Wardric, Deormund, you will come with me to meet the archdeacon. The others will wait outside until we return."

Deormund led Mistig to Ingulf, whom he had befriended in Faversham. "Stay with Ingulf, boy, be good!" The hound obediently sat next to the warrior to watch his master disappear into the palace.

Inside, many Kentish noblemen gathered around a large wooden throne, where a disappointingly ordinary-looking man presided over the gathering. The thin-faced archdeacon, slight of build, made to look smaller by the wide, carved seat, was dressed in a plain green tunic and white breeches. The only signs of his importance were a large silver cross resting on his chest and a broad gold ring inset with a red gemstone, which sparkled as he waved a sheet of parchment above his head.

"This, my lords, is a letter from the scholar Alcuin, arrived from the court of the Frankish Emperor, known to most as Charles the Great. It is addressed to the clergy and nobles of Kent. Listen to his words." The archdeacon lowered the page, cleared his throat and began to read, translating from the Latin with ease:

"A very great danger threatens this island and the people dwelling in it. Behold a thing never before heard of, a pagan people is becoming accustomed to laying waste our shores with piratical robbery." The archdeacon looked around the strained faces. "The letter continues to warn us, dear brethren, that we must amend our ways or be punished. First, we must restore archbishop Aethelhard to his see. We shall be overwhelmed by pagan attackers if we do not reform. We must not be caught unprepared."

Deormund nodded, more to himself. Wasn't that why he had travelled to Thegn Sibert? He, for one, would not be found unready by seaborne raiders if he could help it. But what was the archdeacon saying? What had happened to the archbishop? His thoughts had strayed.

"... attacks on the Gaelic churches of Iona, Inishmurray, Inisbofin and Lambay." The names meant nothing to Deormund, but they were churches; he knew what they were even if he only attended services infrequently. There was one on the high ground of Sceapig at Minster. "Just last month," the prelate's voice rose almost to a scream, "the pagans raided Holmpatrick in Dublin Bay." Again, the names meant nothing, but he heard the word "Ireland" being murmured around him, accompanied by much sage head-shaking. Ireland, he knew, was another kingdom not far from their own, rather like Frankia.

"We must take precautions!" The churchman's thin face twisted into a mask of anger and righteous outrage. "We have an obligation to raise an army, repair bridges and build new ones so that we can move men quickly. We will have to build fortresses and garrison them. From Frankia comes news that the Vikings have established camps whence they exchange goods and captives for ransom." He paused, to glare around with piercing blue eyes, gauging the effect of his words. The prelate need not have worried about the gathered landowners not taking his warnings seriously. The threat was all too credible and a general fear had developed among the many worthies present who stood to lose their traditional wealth.

"My lords," continued the archdeacon, "we must shoulder a common burden. I am making arrangements to sell five sulungs of Church estates near the port of Sondwic, which will permit me to buy a similar hideage close to Canterbury. I am sacrificing a sulung of land—aye, an additional hundred and twenty acres of prime estate—to make this exchange happen. Why? You may well ask! The terrain near Sondwic is strategic, located at the old Roman road that links Dover to Richborough Fortress. The Church cannot defend that land from the Vikings, but the buyer, an ealdorman standing here among you, can." Curious faces turned to stare inquiringly at their neighbours. "We must all make sacrifices. Woe betides those who ignore the peril! Meet together, brothers, make plans to raise an army, to build bridges, to provide strongholds!" The prelate drove home his repetitious message.

It all made sound sense to Deormund, as he told Wardric, whilst the thegn spoke to another landowner next to him.

"Ay, friend Deormund, the Vikings attacked my home town in Dorset last autumn. The Norsemen are becoming a scourge, so we must halt them. You did well to seek out Lord Sibert to learn to fight. I fear we shall all be honing our weapons soon enough.

SEVEN
CANTERBURY
798 AD

The meeting with Archdeacon Wulfred left as many questions unanswered as answered for Deormund. As they rode north, heading for Faversham, he tried to understand what he had heard, but with Thegn Sibert deep in conversation with Wardric, he had nobody to consult. For reasons unknown to him, the Archbishop of Canterbury was in exile and the archdeacon, Wulfred, in some way was standing in for him. Much of the archdeacon's speech made sense to him, but on his island of Sceapig, little news reached his ears of the politics of the age. However, sooner than expected, answers would come.

Their party consisted of twelve horsemen, for whom the journey of just under four leagues, passing through the Forest of Blean, could be easily accomplished in one day: unless something untoward occurred. A more regular and skilled horseman than Deormund might have detected his mount's restlessness and put him on alert. Instead, when they cantered into a clearing, they were surrounded by scores of horsemen armed with spears.

"Sheath it!" Wardric hissed at the deer herder who had drawn his sword in panic. "We cannot resist so many."

Deormund, seeing the hopelessness of their situation, obeyed.

One of the surrounding force rode forward, a nobleman, judging by the gold glinting on his arms and chest.

"Who are you and where are you bound?" His accent marked him as an outsider, and his tone as a man of authority.

"I am Thegn Sibert of Faversham, and these are my liegemen. We are returning home from a meeting in Canterbury. Who are you? Do you mean us harm?"

"We are from Mercia. I am the king's brother—"

"My Lord." The thegn bowed his head and Deormund thought it wise to do likewise.

"And that is my point," the Mercian prince continued. "Are you faithful subjects of King Coenwulf, or was your meeting in Canterbury yet another act of treason in favour of the usurper, Eadberht Praen?"

The thegn squared his shoulders, sitting upright in his saddle. "Nay, Lord, we were in Canterbury at the behest of the Archdeacon of Christ Church, to decide how best to deal with the threat of the Northmen."

"What proof do you have, Thegn?"

"Only my word, Lord, except—"

Deormund gazed anxiously around the glade, where a ring of sharply-pointed spearheads menaced like the teeth of some unimaginable monster, famished, standing ready to pounce and devour them. How could Sibert prove his words?

"Except?" repeated the Mercian prince.

Shocked to hear his name, Deormund barely understood that he was being called upon.

"Deormund, ride forward and show your sword to the

prince. This man slew the Viking chieftain who led a raid on Sceapig. He took the slain warrior's weapon for himself."

"Let me see it!" A sudden silence, stilling the murmuring among the surrounding warriors, greeted the command.

Deormund drew the sword and, careful to bear it unthreateningly with hands under the blade, passed it to the Mercian. The leader of the Mercian army in Kent studied the runic symbols and craftsmanship with narrowed eyes. At last, he handed back the weapon, saying, "This is a Viking blade of fine quality. You speak the truth, Thegn. It is well for you, as we have the usurper in our encampment and instructions not to attack Canterbury. You will come with us to witness the wrath of King Coelwulf."

The Mercian waved to Sibert to join him, waiting until he rode level before wheeling his steed and leading the Kentish man out of the clearing. Deormund geed his horse forward to follow Wardric and the others of his party, with Mistig loping alongside. The Mercians funnelled into the clearing to ride behind them, the deer herder occasionally meeting the glances cast his way and noting respect in their eyes. Undoubtedly, these warriors had heard the claim that he had slain a Viking chieftain. They were not to know that his triumph had come through a well-aimed missile, not the strength of his arm or skill in wielding a sword. He hoped that they would never discover the truth.

"You have proved useful to us once again, deer herder," Wardric muttered, his Dorset burr pleasant to Deormund's ear. "The Mercians have captured King Eadberht, which means they have slaughtered good men of Kent. But for your sword, we may have met the same fate. We still might! They returned your weapon, but don't be deceived; we are their prisoners."

Ahead of them, Prince Wigstan explained to Sibert, "We are on our way to London with the usurper, Eadberht, an enemy of my family. We knew the traitor came over two springs ago from the court of the Frankish Emperor, who hoped to profit from having his puppet installed in Kent. My brother, King Ceolwulf, sent envoys to Pope Leo in Rome. The result is that the scoundrel is excommunicated by virtue of once being a priest. He sought refuge in the great marsh to the south among the ceorls, but we slaughtered them and seized the wretch. To teach the men of Kent loyalty to Mercia, we ravaged the land between Romney and Canterbury. What you will next witness, Thegn Sibert, you will refer to your fellow countrymen as an exhortation to their good faith."

True to this admonition, Deormund learnt from Siward of this conversation later. Meanwhile, they rode on, the deer herder recognising landmarks in the forest and growing aware that, curiously, they were approaching Faversham: their intended destination. They reached the rise to Boughton Hill, where they trotted the horses to the top, the location of a well-chosen, easily defensible encampment.

"Dismount!" ordered Prince Wigstan. Owing to a few hand gestures, once again, they found themselves inside a ring of steel. "Kneel! You are to swear loyalty to King Coelwulf or share the fate of the usurper."

"Speaking for myself," cried Thegn Sibert, "I have never, and would never, rebel against the King. I swear fealty to King Coelwulf."

"I, too," Wardric said in a strong voice.

Deormund wondered what the fate of the captive would be, but copied the thegn and the veteran warrior. "I, too, avow loyalty to King Coelwulf!" he shouted. He asked himself why a Mercian should rule over Kent, but, knowing nothing of politics, he had no regrets about his oath.

"You may rise, friends." Prince Wigstan raised an open hand to signal his words. He turned to a burly warrior, maybe a bodyguard, judging by his stature. "Fetch the so-called King Eadberht!" The prince turned to ask a question in a low voice, meaning that Deormund could not catch his words. A warrior pointed behind them, inducing the Mercian leader to issue another command to Thegn Sibert. "Come this way!" The thegn followed with his small band behind him.

The procession stopped by a campfire while Wigstan issued further instructions in a low voice before waiting with folded arms, studying the expressions on the faces of the Kentish men. Deormund's countenance was relaxed and thoughtful, which it would not have been, had he known that he was about to pass the worst minutes of his life up to now.

A man wearing a leather apron and jerkin, surely a smith, arrived and thrust an iron bar into the glowing embers. Another came bearing a heavy log, bowed, and dropped it at Wigstan's feet. The deer herder felt uneasy, without knowing why.

"Ah! Here is the traitor!" The Mercian prince pointed to a man who was stripped to the waist, his hands bound behind him and led by a cord leash that was noosed around the neck. To make Deormund uneasier still, Mistig, seated dutifully beside him, began a gentle whining. What had the hound sensed? The answer came swiftly, for Wigstan announced, "Men of Kent, behold what fate befalls those who seek to take what is rightfully not theirs."

A swift gesture led to the poor captive being forced to his knees by the giant warrior. Another signal and a different Mercian took the prisoner's hand, stretching the arm over the log. An axeman strode over and raised the blade, bringing it down to sever the hand from the wrist. The screams of the noble victim did not placate the Mercian, also of royal blood. Deormund gazed in incredulous horror as the other hand met the same fate. Merciless and unmoved, the prince ordered the wounds to be cauterised to staunch the bleeding. His senses reeling, the deer herder swayed on his feet, fearing that he would swoon and become the subject of ridicule among the assembled warriors. Weak and dizzy, he did not sense Mistig dash away from the scene of the atrocity. Nostrils assailed by the stench of charred flesh, Deormund's gorge rose, but he was not sick. The ordeal was not yet over, despite the iron being replaced in the fire. Men wound linen strips around the victim's arms and tied them off at the stumps.

"You will never again threaten Mercia or its lands, wretch!" Wigstan gazed into the pallid face of the mutilated man. "You will live to endure a fate worse than death for your crime. Do it!" he commanded.

Realisation dawned on Deormund, who could not bear to look, so covered his eyes with his hand. At another command, a Mercian warrior strode over, snatched his hand away and bent it behind his back. A strong hand grasped the back of his neck, forcing him to watch as the red-hot iron was held the width of a barley grain from Eadberht's eye, blinding it on the instant. The howls of the victim continued, as the operation was repeated in front of the unfortunate's other eye. Sightless and mutilated, he collapsed to the ground where he lay trembling and moaning.

"Cover him with a sheepskin!"

These words came as the first and only sign of humanity—an almost useless deed. Deormund considered what he had witnessed. Having left Sceapig to improve his chances of resisting seaborne raiders, he now understood that whatever existed beyond his island home was no more compassionate than the Northmen he so feared.

If I hadn't sworn fealty to a people I had heard next to nothing about before today, they'd have blinded me, too. Should I just go back home? What if the Vikings come?

"Is that your hound? How come you to have such a creature?"

Mistig had returned, sitting next to his left leg. Deormund came out of his trance and gazed into the visage of the Mercian prince.

"Ay, it is mine, Lord, Mistig helps me with my work."

"Mistig! I like that, for he is as grey as mist! What is your work, fellow?"

"Sire, I am a deer herder. I trap and breed them, organise hunts and carve antlers."

The prince smiled and conceded, "It is all honest work. I adore hunting the deer."

In a display of courage, the prince flung his arms around the ferocious Mistig and stroked him with fondness. Wigstan looked up, smiling. "I love hounds; I have four in my palace at Tomtun." Mistig pressed into the nobleman's chest and his tail beat the ground. The prince stood and declared, "It is a fine hound."

Deormund remained speechless, bemused. *What is the true nature of this man?*

The deer herder had some deep and serious thinking to do, most of which occurred on the short ride to Faversham as he listened to the thegn and the veteran warrior exchanging views on what they had witnessed. Unlike him, both men were battle-hardened. From what he could gather from their words, they had seen sights far worse than the atrocious punishment he had been forced to watch an hour before. Also, the two men accepted the righteousness of the retribution.

Thegn Sibert declared, "A man may not rise and take up arms against his rightful lord. The condemnation is death. Prince Wigstan is loyal to his brother and has shown mercy to Eadberht this day, for he has spared his life."

What life can he have now? I'd rather be dead than living as a blind cripple.

When he had a chance to speak with Lord Sibert alone in Faversham, he would ask him whether the Mercians, as over-lords of Kent, would come to fight and defend their kingdom against its enemies.

That evening at the thegn's table, he learnt that the Mercian King was interested only in the silver obtained from his rights to the royal mint, the markets and royal minsters. They were the main reasons for claiming overlordship. Thinking back to the market at Canterbury and imagining all the markets in Kent, Deormund could understand the benefits accruing. He also learnt that the thegn would renew the defences of Faversham with the help of other local nobles who had attended the archdeacon's meeting.

"Soon, Archbishop Aethelhard will return to Canterbury since he is in the favour of Coelwulf and Pope Leo III," Sibert said. "We must do everything we can to strengthen the king-dom. The archdeacon is right. If the Vikings are attacking Frankia, Frisia and Ireland, they will raid our shores, too. We must repair and build bridges, fortresses and hone our swords. Ah, by the way, Wardric, you will begin instructing our young friend in swordsmanship on the morrow."

"Ay, Lord, we owe him that much."

Suddenly, Deormund had lost all desire to return home. This world without sense was beginning to make sense to him.

EIGHT
FAVERSHAM
798-799 AD

WHEN INSTRUCTING OR ISSUING COMMANDS, WARDRIC'S pleasant Dorset burr disappeared, replaced by an intense edginess that held the listener's attention.

"Heed me well, Deormund, I can do little about your strength of arm, it's something you must work on alone, nor can I address your courage—either you have it, or you don't. That's what you need in a shield-wall, lad: strength and courage. But there is one more thing. It's vital. Can you guess what it is?"

Standing with shield half-raised and wooden practice sword dangling from his arm for a most welcome rest, Deormund nodded his head and uttered a single word, "Swordsmanship."

"Pah! Depends on what you mean by that. If it's what I think, you're wrong. See, I can teach you the moves to defend yourself and to attack with a sword but, useful as that is, it won't make you the fighter I want you to be. Nay, my lad," the veteran warrior grinned, "the essential knack is *cunning*. Get ready. I'll show you."

The two men circled, their shields and practice swords

raised. Suddenly, Wardric lunged and twisted, the mock weapon rapping Deormund behind the knee.

"There you are: cunning, see? With a real blade, your sinews are sliced and you will fall. You are on the ground at my mercy."

"My sinews are on fire. I can't stand, as it is." Deormund hobbled to sit on the edge of a water trough in the thegn's courtyard. "But I see what you mean; feint and attack under the shield."

"Good. Not just under the shield, lad, anywhere you trick the opponent." Wardric approached the trough, stood in front of his pupil and began to dance lightly on his feet: an impressive display for a man of his years. "Lithe on your feet, but it's your eyes that have to be the nimblest. First, observe whether your foe is right- or cack-handed. You can't feint in the same direction when faced by a left-hander or he'll skewer you." A rapid demonstration followed. "If I go this way to a right-hander then swiftly reverse the shift, his flank is exposed. The opposite move for a left-hander, got it?"

Deormund, a quick learner, understood. He sprang to his feet but found that his right leg buckled, causing him to use his sword as a crutch to avoid falling.

"Not today, lad. On the morrow, we'll try out the moves. I'll bring young Milgast; he's another of my pupils, cack-handed as well as guileful. He'll test you to the limits."

Two months of receiving bruises passed until his body resembled that of a dappled fawn, before Wardric declared, "Nobody's breached your guard for three days, lad. I can do no more for you, but don't consider yourself a warrior yet. You've shown me you have the courage, but you need to work on your arm strength."

The relief Deormund felt at reaching the end of his coaching came mixed with a tinge of sadness. Released from the sessions, he could now return to Sceapig to resume his occupation as a deer herder. There would be plenty for him to do with the mating season approaching. More than once, in the past, he had tended the wounds of a defeated stag. This year, there could be only one outcome. The contest should be ill-matched as the hart, if wise, would yield to the younger stag before shedding blood. He loved his work on Sceapig, so why did he feel reluctant to leave Faversham? When he pondered his feelings, he realised that he had tasted a different life, less solitary: one of comradeship. Even the wily Milgast, who had mottled his flesh with bruises, had become a close friend. Living in Faversham also allowed spending cosy evenings with Cynebald, his wife and the girls: his nieces. The more he thought about it, the clearer it became that he would hence-forth divide his time between Sceapig and his parents, and Faversham with his brothers, for Eored was within walking distance at Oare. Now he was married to Saewynn, it might not be long before they presented him with another niece, or even, why not, his first nephew?

Mistig, undoubtedly, was the more excited of the two as they stepped off the ferry to head home on Sceapig. Gradually, the familiar landmarks raised Deormund's spirits, making him remember why he had left the island in the first place. As a herald, Mistig did an impressive job; his scratching and whining at the door while Deormund was still a quarter of a mile away, brought the herder's mother, dishevelled from her chores, running to greet him. Catching her in his arms, the residue of sadness at leaving Faversham evaporated. As mothers will, Bebbe pushed her son to arm's length, scrutinised him and pronounced her satisfaction. "You look strong and well. I'll wager you have an appetite for my eel pie."

Easily resuming his previous occupation, Deormund found an injured hind. The doe had a broken leg, which occasionally happened when misplacing a limb in a burrow when in flight. To spare the animal further pain, and to replenish his mother's larder, he cut the animal's throat without scaring the creature. Hoisting the beast over his shoulders to carry it home, he recalled Wardric's advice to build up his arm strength. Stronger muscles would help in this line of work, too; he smiled wryly at the thought.

With this in mind, he divided his activities between looking after the deer and exercising to increase his muscle bulk. The latter, he did away from prying eyes, by which he meant his mother's. She tended to fuss unnecessarily, so he went to the Ness Forest, found boulders of various sizes and used them, progressively increasing the weight, for lifting. The result surprised him, because not only did his arms become strong, but his thighs and back benefited, too. To complete his exercises, he chose a sturdy branch a yard above head-height. Springing up to catch it with both hands, he used it to pull up his body weight repeatedly, counting his efforts. At first, he could do no more than fifteen, but after a few days he reached fifty, then a hundred.

Naturally, the effect on his physique did not escape Bebbe's hawk-like scrutiny.

"Mother," he explained, "if the Vikings return, I want to be ready for them. I have learnt to wield this," he touched the hilt of his sword with a smile that sent shivers up her spine. "The next time they come to Sceapig, they will pay a high price for my deer."

She looked stricken. "Do you think they will come back?"

"Mother, do not the starlings return to your vegetable seeds?"

The days passed comfortably with his routines and in the loving bosom of his family until, one morning in October, the expected grunts of the stag reached his ears. The rut season had begun. Again, as he had foreseen, the hart did not resist the vigour of his younger rival, making only a token show of his antler prowess before trotting off a discreet distance in surrender. This was the cue for Deormund to snarl him with a rope and lead him to the small compound near his home. There was method in this because, in the rutting season, the males could become unpredictable and he wanted no sly injury to his dominant stag. He would reward the hart for his years of service by bringing him the comfort of two or three hinds. Here in the pen, there would be no complications, simply a guarantee of more calves.

———

THE RUT SEASON OVER, Deormund considered the advisability of crossing the Swale before winter made the trip perilous. He missed his friends and family on the other side of the Channel. Besides, he wanted to test his newly-acquired muscles on Milgast and Wardric, especially him, his veteran tutor, for his approval.

The ferryman, on request, took him right into Oare Creek. A visit to Eored and Saewynn appealed to him before engaging with his friends in Faversham. Two surprises awaited him at the wheelwright's house. Both were pleasant revelations; the first was the unmistakable roundness of Saewynn's figure. When taking her in a greeting embrace, Deormund whispered in her ear, "Are you expecting a babe, sister?" Her radiant smile was all the answer he needed. "Make it a nephew, I have two nieces already."

"You'll take what God has decreed, Deormund."

"Well, I suppose a daughter as pretty as the mother wouldn't come amiss."

"Flatterer! Are you going to linger on the threshold all morning?"

Deormund laughed, then asked, "Where is the father-to-be?"

"Delivering a cart to a farmstead near Hernhill, by the wooden church."

"Ay, I passed that way earlier in the year."

She frowned, considering the distance, calculated and said, "Eored won't be home till late afternoon, I reckon. So, are you coming in or not?" She looked him up and down. "There's something different about you, but what?"

He chose not to tell her. How could he boast about his iron muscles to his brother's wife?

Indoors came the second pleasant surprise. Sitting in a chair by the hearth was an attractive maiden with thick, wavy reddish-brown hair. Her green eyes scrutinised him as he entered the room.

"Cyneflaed, this is my husband's brother. Deormund, she's my cousin, my father's brother's daughter."

"So, this is the deer herder," said the young woman, not more than a score of winters to her years.

"Ay, that I am," he said gruffly, feeling somewhat tongue-tied under the unwavering gaze and fixed smile of the maiden. "What does your father do?"

She smiled, replying enigmatically, "The same as Saewynn's father."

"A miller? But there's only one mill in Faversham."

"You are observant, deer herder," she replied tartly. "And yet, my father is a miller."

Perplexed and mildly irritated, Deormund asked, "So where is your father's mill?"

"About ten leagues to the west. Do you know Ebbsfleet? The mill is in the valley. It is a tidal mill, Father has fish ponds there, too." There was no mistaking the note of pride in her voice.

"So, what brings you to Faversham?"

She pouted, making him wonder if he had been awkward. Clumsiness would be understandable, since he had not sought out female company at all in his five-and-twenty years. Yet, there sat a lovely young woman whose presence, he realised, might change that attitude.

Finally, she replied, "I have two sisters and two brothers, all younger. Although the mill prospers, so many hungry mouths are a burden. Father sent me into service, here in Faversham, in Thegn Sibert's household. Today, I am free and so I came to see my cousin—I'm glad I did!" She tilted her head and smiled.

Teased, his heart skipped whilst his cheeks burnt.

"Come, sit by me and tell me all about deer. I love looking at them in paintings and tapestries but I've never seen one in real life. They never come near the mill," she added sorrowfully.

"When is your next free day, Cyneflaed? We can take the ferry to Sceapig where you'll see as many as your heart desires."

"Really!" She sprang to her feet. "Did you hear that, Saewynn? Deormund will show me his deer! Will they have real horns?"

"Antlers? Ay, the males will."

She delighted him with her excited countenance. "This day next week. I'll be free all day."

She was having a strange effect on his heart. It was thumping madly. Without thinking, he blurted, "I'll come for you an hour after dawn. We'll go to the crossing point straightaway."

Suddenly, he looked sorrowful.

"Is something the matter?"

Her gentle concern bothered him. Embarrassed and flushing, he said, "Nothing. Except I don't think that I can survive a whole week without seeing you again."

She laughed gaily, a delightful, throaty sound that set him a-tingle. What was happening to him?

"Nonsense, deer herder, you hardly know me! Was your Eodred like this, Saewynn?"

The other woman walked over, put her mouth to Cyneflaed's ear and breathed something into it. The green eyes moved to his face, burning red with shame. "I'll bear that in mind," she said and smiled sweetly at him. "Do you know the thegn? You could find an excuse to seek me in his hall. I'll be about my duties, unable to chat idly."

Deormund intended to find Wardric there, but realising that he'd already made his feelings for her clear enough, merely nodded. The arrival of Eored put a welcome end to the mismanagement of his new-found amorousness. The two men had much catching up to do, whilst the women bustled about preparing a meal and casting surreptitious glances at the brothers, which were not lost on the stalker's keen eye.

After eating, Cyneflaed said she had to return to the hall. Twilight was approaching, so Deormund offered to walk with her. Again, he did not fail to catch the exchanged glances of the two women. They set off at once, Cyneflaed chattering happily about the planned visit to see the deer.

Perhaps luckily, neither noticed the figure of a man with a thunderous expression lurking in the shadows of the deserted twilit street.

NINE
FAVERSHAM, KENT
799 AD

INSTEAD OF FINDING FRIENDS ON HIS VISIT TO THE thegn's hall, on the contrary, Deormund discovered an enemy. With no sign of Wardric or Milgast, he spent time gazing around in search of Cyneflaed. When he chanced to sight her, their eyes met and she gave him a pretty smile but hurried away, concerned to fulfil her duties. The exchange of glances had not gone unnoticed.

A burly fellow, taller than Deormund, approached the deer herder.

"Oi, you!" he said roughly, his voice conditioned by a defect, a cleft palate that deformed the unfortunate man's upper lip and ran up to his nostrils. The blemish, tainting him since birth, would not alone have made him exceedingly ugly. That was achieved by his aggressive expression as he uttered, "I want a word with you!"

At first, Deormund thought there must be some mistake, so he turned to look behind him to see who the man was addressing.

"It's you I want to talk to!" The man, with the stature of a warrior, seized the herder's arm and pulled him around to face his belligerent visage.

"Do I know you?"

"Nay, and you don't want to! You stay away from my betrothed or it'll be the worst for you, understand?"

Confused, Deormund looked into the close-set dark eyes of the taller man and tried frantically to grasp what had been said.

"Cyneflaed? Your betrothed? She didn't tell me she was spoken for."

"Ay, well, she is, so you stay away from her, do you hear?" He accompanied these words by tightening his grip on Deormund's arm until it was tight as a vice. A few months before, the deer herder would have cried out in pain, but now his muscles were hardened; he saw by the other's troubled expression that he had noted his strength.

"Unhand me!" Deormund's eyes flashed a challenge directly into the pugnacious visage. Not to be cowed, the fellow transformed the grip into a shove, causing Deormund to stagger backwards. His hand went to his sword hilt, but the man was already walking away; in any case, the deer herder noted the absence of a weapon at his belt. He stood, staring after the retreating back.

Cyneflaed betrothed? Just my luck!

Standing in gloomy silence, he felt another tug at his sleeve. "Cyneflaed!"

She gazed anxiously into his face, her eyes seeking answers to an as yet unspoken questions.

"What did that brute want of you?"

"To warn me off associating with you."

"What! How dare he?"

"He says you are betrothed, Cyneflaed. Why did you not tell me?"

She glared at him. "Because it is a lie! That monster stalks

68

me and will not leave me be. Oh, Deormund, I fear he will harm me."

Deormund's mind was racing, rage seething apace. Cyneflaed was *his* beloved and no man would pester her and live to tell the tale. His eyes left her distraught face, now wet with tears, and swept around the vast, beamed room. He saw him then, in a far corner, his eyes fixed on him and the maiden. An initial reaction was to rush across and have it out with the rogue, but Cyneflaed's tear-filled eyes halted him. He would not leave her without reassurances.

"Nobody will harm you, Cyneflaed. You have my word on that!"

"But, my sweet, he is one of Thegn Sibert's bodyguards. He's a dangerous brute. Have a care!"

"Nay, he's the one who must be wary. I'll not have him frighten you."

Her lower lip trembled, "H-he says he'll have me one way or another. I'd rather drown in Father's mill pond!"

"Enough of that talk! It's a sin to take your life. Besides, how can I live without you?"

At last, a glimmer of a smile, fleeting but seen by Deormund,

"Thegn Sibert is a friend; I'll speak with him about your situation. Only today, I have not seen him, or any of my friends for that matter. I wanted to have a word with Wardric."

"Deormund, I must return to work. Have a care!"

She surprised him by giving him a light kiss on the cheek. Unable to help himself, his eye swept to the far corner, but the hulking figure of the warrior had vanished. As he watched Cyneflaed hasten away, he admitted to himself that he'd prefer the menacing fellow not to have seen the peck on his face. At the same time, he simmered at the thought of Cyneflaed's tears.

Since, for some inexplicable reason, the thegn and his

friends were not in the hall, there was no point in wasting the morning even if every glimpse of his beloved was precious. Deciding to return to his brother's house because he needed to confide in someone he trusted, Deormund strode out of the door and hurried on his way.

Stepping out of an alleyway, a tall, burly figure cried, "Oi, you!"

Not again! He'll get more than he bargained for.

At this thought, Deormund drew his sword and stood ready as the warrior approached.

"I thought I told you to stay away from my betrothed!"

The menace was clearer than the indistinct words, so Deormund stepped forward, regardless of the other man being unarmed. The tip of his blade pressed into the flesh of the fellow's throat, causing his eyes to bulge with rage and fear.

"Coward! Will you slay a defenceless man?" Saliva drooled from the corner of the deformed mouth.

Deormund pushed his blade a little harder and saw a thin rivulet of blood run down the slack skin.

"Cyneflaed tells me that you are not betrothed and that she doesn't want you. So, you'll stay away from her or else you'll have me to reckon with, not to mention my friend, Thegn Sibert."

The narrowed eyes studied him warily as the warrior took a step back from the tormenting weapon. "I dread no *deer herder!*" The distorted words nonetheless conveyed the mocking tone. "I know the thegn better than you, fool!"

"I care nothing for your filthy life and fear no man in combat. Go, run! Fetch a blade, we'll finish this." Even as the words left his mouth, he realised the folly.

Like two stags rutting over a hind.

The uncouth indistinct voice growled, "I've warned you to stay away from *my* betrothed. Be it on your own head now!"

The hulking brute turned to disappear down the alleyway whence he had emerged. Deormund did not know where the ginnel led, nor did he care. Maybe he should have taken more notice. Striding towards his brother's home, faster than he needed, unconsciously putting distance between himself and the unsavoury character, his enemy's warning still rang in his ears. Like it or not, they had unfinished business. As he told Cynebald later, a fight would be inevitable if the scoundrel importuned Cyneflaed again.

His brother tried to reason with him. Slaying the warrior would lead to problems with the law. At the very least, he would have to find a substantial wergild for a thegn's body-guard. Such a fine was beyond a deer herder's means. Not paying it would incur an exemplary punishment: something severe.

"Nay, Deormund, if you cannot do without the maiden, it would be better to speak with Thegn Sibert. Explain the situation and leave it to him to deal with this rogue."

Despite a series of *what-ifs* tormenting his mind, he agreed with his brother's sage advice and set off the next morning determined to follow it. Even so, as a precaution, he carried his shield with him. A wise decision, he felt. *Better to be on the safe side.* And so it proved because, along his way, out of the same alleyway emerged the warrior, who had been waiting for him. This time, he was carrying a sword and shield, too. Worse still, behind him followed two other similar giants, brandishing swords.

Now who's the coward? By God, three against one! These will be other bodyguards.

He came to a halt and eyed the harelipped warrior with loathing and drew his weapon, cursing his luck that he could not follow Cynebald's counsel. But if he had to die here for the love of Cyneflaed, so be it!

The brute was prepared to give him an honourable way out.

"On your knees, deer herder, swear you will stay away from my betrothed."

"I can't do that, fellow, for she is not betrothed to anyone, not even to me."

"Either make the vow or lose your life here!"

"So be it!" Deormund raised his shield and prepared for the assault. He assumed it would come from three adversaries, but having cursed his luck earlier, now, he ought to have blessed it. Eyes only on his opponent, he did not realise the change in his fortunes. He was still registering that his foe was right-handed and, making his calculations accordingly, he deflected a savage blow with his shield to lunge into a thrust that was equally parried. His antagonist was a skilled fighter, but he had already assumed as much. Again, he warded off a strike, but, remembering Wardric's coaching, feinted twice and obtained some result. Not enough, unfortunately, because the nick inflicted on the hulking warrior's sword arm was superficial, enough to draw blood and enrage, but not incapacitate him.

The wearying sequence of blows and countering, feinting and dodging, continued. The distraction of a scream from behind him broke the warrior's concentration. The split-second proved fatal as Deormund's blade slashed his adversary's throat. Surprise and shock, hatred and fear: Deormund read the sequence as his foe sagged to the ground. Spinning around, fearing an attack on his back, he gasped in amazement as his incredulous gaze took in an unexpected sight: the body of one of the other huge warriors lay crumpled and bloodied on the street. Two men were fighting the other giant. A mixture of astonishment and joy swept through him as he realised that his saviours were no other than Wardric and Milgast.

He hastened towards the struggle and yelled, "Hold! For

now, it is three against one, and I have no quarrel with this man."

"Do you yield," Wardric asked, "or will you end up like your comrades? Food for scavengers?"

The giant looked from Wardric to Milgast and then at the nearing Deormund. "I yield! It was never my quarrel in the first place."

"Nay, but you disappoint me, Eadlac," Wardric growled, "for you find yourself in the circumstances you wanted to put our friend in: three on one. I dare say you and your cronies would not have shown the deer hunter the same mercy he offers you."

"We should go to Thegn Sibert and explain these deaths to him," Milgast said. "Sheath your sword, Eadlac."

The hulking warrior did as bid, casting an eye over his dead comrades. "We can't just leave them here," he muttered.

"Ay, you have the right of it!" Wardric agreed. "Deormund, Milgast, take his arms and legs!" He indicated the body with the cleft lip. "You," he ordered the bodyguard, "help me with this one, grasp under his knees!"

With considerable effort, they carried the dead weights to the thegn's hall, where, after a heated discussion with the guard at the door, they dumped the bodies on the floor amid the freshly-strewn scented reeds.

Thegn Sibert hurried to the scene. "What is the meaning of this?" He stared aghast at the grotesque corpses.

Deormund gazed anxiously at the thegn; he knew there would be a price to be paid for the deaths of two of the lord's bodyguards.

The highest-ranking among the men present, the veteran Wardric, spoke first.

"Lord, Milgast and I were advised by one of your servants... a girl, that this man," he pointed at the body of Deormund's enemy, "and his two cronies would waylay Deormund to slay him in a dispute over that same girl. She overheard their scheme and rushed to advise me, knowing that Deormund is my friend."

Thegn Sibert's countenance had become puce with rage. He turned his face on the surviving warrior. "Is this true, Eadlac?"

Desperation on his face, the man nodded. "I fear it is so, Lord. I only wanted to help Dombert," he nodded towards the body of the harelipped brute.

"Three of my best men against yon deer herder?" The thegn's incredulous voice rose to a roar. The nobleman spun around. "What do you have to say about this?" He glared at Deormund, his tone furious.

"It is the truth, Lord. That fellow Dombert had threatened me twice, nay, thrice, to stay away from his betrothed. But it wasn't true, they were not pledged. He had but cast lustful eyes upon Cyneflaed, and since he wanted her, he decided to rid himself of me—his rival."

"Fetch the maid!" The thegn fairly bellowed the words. There was no need, as she came running on hearing the command.

"Sire, I am here!" she panted, casting a wide-eyed gaze at Deormund.

The thegn now spoke gently. "Girl, you are not in trouble. Tell me what you overheard these men saying."

She glared at the body of Dombert and pointed. "All his fault! He'd been pestering me, Lord, since I came to work here. The ugly brute said he would have me one way or another... b-but," she gazed at the deer herder, "but I love Deormund."

"Do you, by God!" The thegn lost patience and his voice hardened. "I asked you to tell me what you overheard."

She flushed, looked stricken, glanced fearfully at the tall

bodyguard, but found the courage to speak. "Dombert asked him and the other one," she pointed at the second corpse, "to help get rid of the deer herder, that's what he said. I knew he meant Deormund. They would waylay him from an alleyway as he came here. They knew he would come. I remembered he told me that wanted to see his friend Wardric, so I thought I'd better reveal the plot to him."

"Ay, that she did, Lord. When the maiden told me there were three of your bodyguard, I sought Milgard, who is also a friend of Deormund, to make it a fair fight—hoping to stop the combat. Although we hastened to the spot the maid had heard, we were only in time to prevent all three from attacking him."

So, that's how it went!

Deormund glanced at Cyneflaed and smiled, then looked at Wardric, saying, "I thank my lucky stars that you arrived when you did. Dombert was a worthy opponent."

"Yet, you defeated him." Everyone looked at Thegn Sibert's face, that showed no sign of his rage abating. "Deer herder, you slew my bodyguard. For that, there is a price to be paid!"

That was what he had feared. Anxiously awaiting the lord's verdict, he bowed his head and stared disconsolately at the reeds mixed with highly-scented dried lavender, that were strewn at his feet.

"This is my decision," the nobleman announced. "You, Deormund, will wed Cyneflaed within the month if she agrees." Deormund raised his head, startled. "Only after the wedding will you enter my service to replace the man you slew. He gazed with contempt at the body of the harelipped warrior. As for you, Eadlac, you will swear before us all that you harbour no grudge against Deormund. Then, you will hie to the graveyard where *you alone* will dig two graves for your comrades. That will be your punishment for your part in this affair. Now, I await two answers." He gazed at Cyneflaed.

She blushed and said, "Ay, bless you, Lord, I will wed Deormund if he will have me."

"I will! And I'll gladly serve as your guard, Thegn."

The satisfied nobleman beamed at the couple as they embraced. Then his smile vanished, to be replaced by a stern expression. "And you?" he addressed his bodyguard.

"Lord, I solemnly swear I never had, and do not now bear, any grudge against Deormund. We will serve as comrades together."

"All's well, then! The four of you will carry the bodies to the graveyard. I will find the priest. Wardric, ensure that Eadlac digs the graves by himself!"

"Ay, Lord!"

Deormund bent to raise the body of Dombert. While doing so, he glanced at Cyneflaed, who was gazing at him with an expression of unconcealed love. As he heaved the arms of his foe, he thought, *To think I was cursing my ill-luck earlier! How wrong a man can be!*

TEN

FAVERSHAM, KENT NOVEMBER

799 - 800 AD

"Lord, most things are in place on Sceapig for my herd. I need a few days there to organise my father for him to take over," his thoughts tumbled out in a torrent of words, "and rectify the structures... oh, and to present my bride to my parents."

The thegn laughed, but his face grew serious.

"First, you bereave me of a guard; now, you wish to deprive me of his replacement!"

Noticing the twinkle in the thegn's eye that betrayed his grave countenance and disclosed his true sentiments, Deormund gave a swift reply.

"Thegn, if you do not concede me time on Sceapig, you will have no deer to chase. It is weaning time, there's work to be done."

"Let's be clear on this, Deormund. I will grant you three days, no more. You and your wife have duties to fulfil here in Faversham and perform them, you *will!* Besides, I will not waive my hunt."

"Thank you, Lord." Deormund bowed, hurrying away to

fetch Cyneflaed. They would make the crossing without delay, that morning.

Their arrival pre-announced by the bounding Mistig, again free to scamper around the familiar scents of his beloved island, resulted, as usual, in Bebbe bursting out to greet her son. This time, though, she stopped in her tracks at the vision of a beautiful maiden with reddish-brown hair grinning at her.

"Mother, meet Cyneflaed!"

Bebbe's heart sang. At last! Her recalcitrant son had found himself a maid. Awkwardly, she said, "Welcome, my dear, to our home. So, Deormund, finally, you are betrothed!"

"Nay, Mother," he replied, pausing long enough to enjoy her discomfited expression, "not betrothed... but *wed!* Come, hug your new daughter."

The astonishment on her face made him grin, but his sentiments became more restrained as he watched the two important women in his life embrace.

"Asculf!" Bebbe cried, unable to contain her excitement, her shout fetching the shepherd at a run from a barn where he had been stacking bales of winter fodder. "Our Deormund is wed! Can you believe it?"

A cosy hour passed as they devoured Bebbe's freshly-baked honey cakes. The women drank Asculf's mead whilst the men supped ale.

"Father, we can only stay two more days." These words were followed by Bebbe's wail of "Oh, no!" accompanied by a possessive grasp of Cyneflaed's hand. "I'm sorry, Mother, but we are both in service to Thegn Sibert. He gave permission for three days on Sceapig... and no more."

"But what about your animals?"

"That, Father, is another reason why we are here. It's weaning time. I will have to rely on your help. First, we will bring the calves to the shed for overwintering and you'll need to feed them. I mean to repair and strengthen the fencing so that you can leave the shed door open. The hinds must be free to roam into the enclosure, otherwise, they tend to bully each other when indoors."

"How will I know how much to feed them? We'll need more fodder. I've provided only enough for the sheep."

"Don't worry. I'll spend a day collecting sea kale—they love that. When it's consumed, you can collect more. I'm sure you'll bring in more hay for them. Consider that each red deer hind needs as much food as two large ewes. Oh, I'll have to prepare the enclosure ground, too; it will need strewing with tree bark. Fortunately, I prepared three full sacks of bark last time I was here."

"You have much to do, son."

"Ay, but Cyneflaed can help strew the bark and lead in the calves. Oh, and Father, I will send you money for your troubles. I know it's more work for you, but I have no choice."

He went on to relate the terrible story of the death of Dombert and the consequent obligation to service.

After careful reflection, Asculf said, "Never fear, my brave warrior, I'll look after your deer." He was proud of the valour of his youngest son.

"I've never seen a baby deer—or a *deer*, for that matter!"

"Don't get too excited, Cyneflaed. You'll soon tire of the beasts!"

"Never!"

"You will!"

"I won't. I swear it!"

Their pleasant interlude over, Deormund carried the sacks to the compound and strewed the ground with bark around his feet. "Spread it like this, love, not too thickly." He positioned the two other large hemp bags to save her tramping back to the same spot to obtain more bark. "We'll bring the deer when you've finished."

She worked happily with this prospect in mind whilst he inspected the wooden fencing. The paling stood taller than Deormund, at six feet six inches, a foot higher. He grunted in satisfaction; he had completed the elrick, or enclosure, the previous year, so the palisade had endured one winter and showed no signs of deterioration. He shoved and kicked any post he thought less sturdy, but all stood the test of his thorough inspection.

Pleased with Cyneflaed's work, he folded the empty sacks and carried them into his father's barn.

"Ready?" he pointlessly asked his exhilarated helper; there was no need for a reply.

Drawing the whistle from his tunic, he put it to his lips to blow one shrill blast. In moments, Mistig was by his side, staring inquisitively at his master.

"Time to round them up, old friend," he told the hound, whose throaty growl he took to mean *understood*.

They hastened to the meadow, where Mistig was already persuading the more distant hinds to congregate centrally.

"Aw, look! Aren't the babies beautiful!"

"*Calves*, Cyneflaed—a deer herder's wife should use the correct term."

"That one's unsteady on its legs."

"Ay, a late arrival. She'll be about three months; the others are around five. I'm afraid you'll have to carry her to the elrick. Don't worry, the calf won't be too heavy. Come, I'll show you how to pick her up."

That accomplished, they trudged, each with a calf in arms, back to the enclosure.

"I'll swear you're more in love with that creature than you are with me, wife."

"Look at these eyes, Deormund! How could anyone not be captivated?"

Mistig's boundless energy and constant harassment ensured that the deer filed obediently into the compound. The herder gratefully closed the gate, knowing that he could rely on his father to care for them over the winter. He considered the work still to do: next, a treat for the hound, then, the last tasks of penning the stags individually, followed by an outing to gather sea kale. The three empty sacks would be handy for that.

When Cyneflaed offered to help with the harvesting, he replied, "I think you should stay at home, get to know Mother a bit better. I can manage," he added gruffly.

He regretted his decision on his final return trip to the shore to fetch the third bulging sack. As with the other two, it was light: the problem was its bulk. Awkward to carry, the bag made him stop several times to readjust the burden. Comforted by the thought that the three sacks would tide his father over until the end of the next month if mixed with hay, he placed the sack in the store, taking a large handful for his mother's cooking pot. Cabbage was all very well, but he much preferred the taste of sea kale.

"I can't believe you've never eaten it, Cyneflaed. Tomorrow, I'll take you to collect some more, so you'll know what to search for. We'll see if we can catch some crabs, too."

On their way to the beach, Cyneflaed confided, "I like your mother, Deormund. You take after her. Did you know, she isn't aware that Saewynn is with child? I didn't say anything; it's better coming from you." He bent forwards, kissing her. "What's that for?"

He pondered his reply then at last, with a fond smile, he said, "Just because you are being you!"

Once their three days were over, Deormund decided to break his brother's news to Bebbe.

"If you'd told me before, I could have crossed to Oare with you," she scolded. "I'd have prepared a meal for your father."

"Go with them, Bebbe. I can fend for myself."

Agreed on this, they set off for the ferryman's hut, where they found Heorstan working on a wicker eel trap.

"About time I replaced the old one," he explained, with a cheery grin. "I expect you'll be going to see Eored's wife." He turned his attention to Bebbe.

"It seems everyone knows... except me," she grumbled, but her heart sang. This fleeting happiness vanished when she glanced at her son's troubled face. "What's the matter, Deormund?"

Not wishing to trouble the others, he muttered a lie. "Nothing, Mother, nothing at all." His worry would keep until he entered the thegn's hall. Only then, would he mention it to Sibert.

Although his heart, like his mother's and wife's, should have been soaring on wings of joy, it was chained to a dungeon floor of his creation. Troubles assume this character, disguising a bad moment to make it appear a lifetime. His worries surfaced when he was alone with his brother.

"Eored, do you have a weapon?"

"Why do you ask?"

"Well, do you?"

"Not unless you'd call my hatchet for chopping wood a weapon." He looked quizzically at Deormund. "I said, why do you ask?"

"I think you should arm yourself. You never know, you may have to defend yourself... or your family."

"Is there something wrong, Deormund? A threat to my family?"

"Nay, I'm sorry. I didn't mean to alarm you, but it wouldn't harm to buy a sword or a battle-axe, would it?"

"Has this anything to do with what happened to you some days ago?"

"Nay, Eored. Or perhaps aye, who knows?" he lied, not wishing to trouble his brother further, adding, "It's true that lately I have been thinking of vulnerability"—and, that much, was not a lie—"so, take it from me, one of Thegn Sibert's bodyguard, you should consider my advice."

Eored scrutinised the earnest face and decided that he was right. The assault on Deormund had shaken his brother's confidence although he wouldn't admit to it. Still, maybe he was right; it would not harm to get his blacksmith friend to forge him a hooked axe-head with a long, curved cutting edge. If it only served as a decoration hanging on the wall, at the least, it would provide reassurance. "All right, I'll have a word with Sherred the smith. As I'm his regular customer, he'll make me a battle-axe at a decent price.

"Good, that's settled then. I'm off to join Cyneflaed and the others."

Eored watched him leave the workshop. He frowned, for he had noticed the look of relief on his brother's face when, he, Eored, had agreed to have a weapon forged. Was there more to his worries than met the eye?

———

IF DEORMUND BELIEVED that his duty at the thegn's hall would be restricted merely to guarding the person of Thegn Sibert, his urgent conversation with the man himself soon disabused him. Assured that Cyneflaed was not within earshot, he approached his lord and master.

"Thegn, yesterday, when we crossed the Swale, I spied a sail out at sea. It was far off, but I reckon it was another Viking vessel. The pirates are back in our waters."

The warrior studied the anxious face of his bodyguard and spoke in a low voice. "They never left our coasts, Deormund. These raiders have a thirst for silver and jewels. I have been in contact with the archdeacon and he, in turn, with kings. I have to raise a force. You see," he confided, "these pirates have been making regular incursions along not only our coastline, but also troubling the Suth Seaxe.

"Their latest activity is to build a fortress, thence to maraud in the surrounding land, taking hostages when they deem someone useful to the purpose, to ransom the captive for silver. If none is forthcoming, they behead the unfortunate and place his head on a sharpened stake as a warning to others. Our coastal monasteries and nunneries are vulnerable, too. Archdeacon Wulfred has received an impassioned plea for protection from Abbess Selethrytha of Lyminge. We leave for the coast tomorrow to ensure the safety of her abbey. Another task will be to demolish or destroy any fortresses constructed by previous raiders so that they cannot be occupied again."

The thegn smiled grimly. "Deormund, you, who slew a Viking chieftain, know that a stout-hearted Saxon is a match for any Norseman. We will avenge the slaughter, rape and pillage if we come across a crew of pirates. Give me a chance and I'll burn their ship, too."

"Ay," growled Deormund, thinking about the safety of his family, "we'll slay the lot of them!"

The thegn grasped his arm and smiled into his face. "You are good man, Deormund. I want you to eat beside me at my table this evening. Your wife will serve our food. Then tonight, you'll say your fond farewells," he grinned suggestively as men alone together will, "for we shall be away till the winter sets in and the pirates are forced elsewhere by the foul weather."

ELEVEN
OARE, KENT
800 AD

THE FORGE DOOR WAS AJAR AS ALWAYS, IN A DESPERATE BID for more air. Sherred was beating an iron bar into the shape of a scythe blade when Eored slipped through the gap. The smith's begrimed face broke into a broad smile at the sight of his customer and friend.

"What brings you here today? More nails, I'm guessing."

Eored beamed. "You're wide of the mark, Sherred. I have a commission for you."

"Oh, aye, no point in beating my poor brain like an iron from the forge." He laid his tongs on the workbench and sat on the anvil, waving at a wooden chest for the wheelwright to sit, too. "There are so many things I could make that it'd take all day to list them and even then, I might not guess what you're after."

Eored laughed but secretly admitted that the smith wasn't bragging, because the renown of his skill had reached beyond neighbouring Faversham.

"Since you know me well, I dare say my request will startle you all the more."

Intrigued, the blacksmith silently began on the list he'd refused to consider, but to no avail. He shook his shaggy blond head. "Let's be having it, then."

The wheelwright gave him a sheepish grin that aroused the smith's curiosity even more. "I want you to fashion me a battle-axe—you know, with a curved blade," his hand traced an arc in the air, "and a hook underneath."

Sherred roared with laughter. "Are you going to war, Eored?"

A sour look greeted the brawny man's mirth. "With these sea wolves circling, Sherred, a man has to look after his family."

"Ay, I heard your family will be bigger soon." The smith leapt off his anvil and hauled a wooden chest from under the bench. Tipping back the lid, he rummaged inside, tossing oddly-shaped implements and unidentifiable pieces of metal onto the beaten-earth floor.

"Something like this?" He produced a wicked-looking axe-head from the chest. The shape conformed exactly to what Eored had in mind. The wheelwright, unlike the smith, had to take the weighty object in both hands to inspect it. The arced rim of the blade had been bevelled on each side to produce a sharp cutting edge, whilst the extremities came to two evil-looking tips.

"Ay, you can use it as a pick as well. Those points will penetrate the thickest skull," the smith said, with a relish that made Eored shudder.

"How come you just happened to have this in your chest?" he asked, as he inspected the iron ring at the back, ready-made for a haft.

"Years ago, I made weapons for the king. When you were young, there was a tussle for the throne. Arrowheads, spear-heads, axe-heads—every bloody head you can name, I made it! This one must have had no taker, so I shoved it under the bench with other odds and ends. All it needs is a good polish and honing."

"It seems well-honed enough to me."

"Ay, well, you can never have a weapon too sharp, can you? You'll need a whetstone if you plan to use it."

"I have more than one whetstone for my chisels."

"Ay, of course. Well, you'll be needing a haft for yon." He strode over to a rack of ash poles and selected one. "This should do nicely, five-foot long."

"As long as that?"

"What kind of warrior will you make, I ask? A five-foot pole means you don't get within the enemy's range, but you strike him. See what I mean?" The flashing staff passed an inch from Eored's startled face.

"I guess you're right!"

"Pass me yon axe." He pointed to the axe-head before selecting a lump hammer. "Put it on the bench."

Eored picked up the piece of steel again, noting its weight, taking it over to lay it beside Sherred, who was tightening the pole in a vice. As if picking up nothing heavier than a dried oak leaf, the smith raised the axe-head and placed the ring over the end of the pole. Grasping his hammer, he crashed it down on the steel, driving it into position with two blows. "Good!" he grunted. "One last thing now."

His thick fingers fumbled with the lid of a small box, from which he extracted metal wedges and laid them in a line on the bench. "This one's about right." The smith's finger and thumb delicately raised a wedge, which he held in front of Eored's nose. "I'll drive this into the haft, making a kerf to ensure your axe-head never flies away when you're wielding it. Imagine that amid a battle!" He roared with laughter at the joke.

The two men agreed on an equitable price; which in reality, in the name of friendship, was favourable to the buyer.

Eored swaggered out of the smithy with the fearsome weapon resting against his shoulder. As he strode home, he smiled grimly at the astonished glances of the folk he passed. One small boy received a cuff around the ear for pestering him to hold the axe.

"Ay, you'd only drop it on your foot because it's too heavy for you to lift. Now scoot along, whilst you've still got both feet to run on!"

Saewynn greeted him with similar incredulity at the sight of his purchase. "Whatever possessed you to buy that? You promised to make a cradle, not to go off on a fool's errand!"

He ignored her and laid the axe on the table, again paying no heed to her scolding—*shift that dreadful thing from my table!* Instead, he brought a hammer and nails from the workshop and drove nails into the wall, positioning them to suspend the weapon.

"There! Better than a tapestry, that."

"Eored," his wife asked uneasily, "what made you spend on that *thing*? You don't think you'll need it, do you?"

Her wide blue eyes and delicate state moved him to tenderness.

"My sweetheart," he said, taking her into a reassuring embrace, "I certainly hope not, but I have to think of my family," he caressed her bulge gently, "with these raiders off our shores, lurking like a pack of wolves ready to pounce on unwary prey. Well, I mean to be prepared."

"Oh, Lord!" she sagged into a chair and looked miserable.

"Sorry, Saewynn, I didn't want to frighten you." He looked around the small room. "Where's Cyneflaed, by the way?"

"Oh, she's gone to the market for me. She said lifting weights in my condition is bad."

"Good lass! She's right about that! Well, I'd better get back to work."

"I'll call you for lunch," she said, not gazing at her husband as she spoke but rather at the fearful object on the wall.

Eored worked hard for three more days whilst, unknown to him, Deormund was engaged in demolishing a Viking fortress near Lyminge. More concerning was that his brother had spotted the striped sail of a longship out at sea, veering into the estuary.

"Thegn Sibert!" His cry revealed his agitation. "Over yonder!" All eyes, not just those of the nobleman, locked onto the pirate vessel. "It's heading towards Faversham, Lord!"

"Leave what you are doing, men," the thegn ordered, to Deormund's satisfaction, "we must reach our town before the Norsemen."

Neither Deormund nor Sibert could know that the Vikings would not get to Faversham but veer into Oare Creek. Cyneflaed discovered that before them. She was handing a silver piece to a poultry trader in exchange for a bag of sparrows when she felt eyes on her. On looking around, she spied the leering face of a tall, blond warrior, his face painted with blue icicles falling fearsomely down his cheeks. She understood at once that he was a Viking. Snatching her change, she hurried up the street to her cousin's house. Fearfully glancing over her shoulder, she saw that the brute was striding after her. With no alternative, she hitched her dress and ran, again darting a fearful glance behind her. The monster was closing on her, a vile grin on his face. She dashed into Saewynn's house, slammed the birds on the table and rushed to grab a long, sharp carving knife.

"Cyneflaed! What's going on?" her cousin asked, but then screamed as the giant warrior burst into the room.

With a sneer, he grabbed Cyneflaed's puny wrist to stay the blade she strove to plunge into his neck. A macabre dance followed as he tried to wrestle her into submission. A most uneven struggle ensued: his powerful muscles against her frail frame. Saewynn's screaming continued but did not befog her thinking. Quick-witted and nimble despite her bulge, she unhooked the pot from its tripod over the fire and flung scalding water into the Norseman's face. Her aim was true, so that now it was he screaming and sinking to his knees, his hands over his injured face, just as Eored burst into the room, alerted by his wife's screams.

The wheelwright swooped to seize the axe off the wall and in a single movement put the Viking out of his misery. Dropping the weapon, he grabbed the legs of the corpse and pulled it to the door. "Open the door, Cyneflaed," he ordered. Still clutching the carving knife, she obeyed, her heart beating wildly in her chest.

She followed Eored outdoors, glanced down the street and, to her horror, saw another Viking hurrying towards them. Weighing up the situation, she dodged around the corner into an alley between the houses before calling to Eored.

"Look out! Another one's coming!"

He swore and declared he would fetch his axe. On the alert, all her senses worked in crazed unison. First, she smelt smoke, then heard screaming from the streets below that lined the harbour. Next, she peered around the edge of the wall and saw the Norseman bent over his dead comrade, his skull cloven by Eored's axe.

"Gudrik!" The cry sounded like the bellow of an enraged bull. Three things happened at once: the Viking straightened, Eored emerged with his battle-axe, and Cyneflaed raced around the corner, leaping upon the raider's back. She grabbed his hair and pulled sharply, slashing the knife across his throat. Shocked, but still efficient, Eored chopped the axe into the warrior's arm, severing it at the elbow. His action was unnecessary because Cyneflaed had already slain him. She screamed as he crumpled, his weight falling on top of her. Eored had to drag the body away to free her.

"Go, look after Saewynn!" He began to run down the street. There were more Vikings to fight.

The sight that greeted him was horrendous. Three houses were ablaze; the smoke swept past him driven by the sea breeze. Almost tripping over the body of a fisherman he knew, he cursed the pirates, their wives and children all to Hell.

The Norsemen might have chosen an easier target than the hardy fishermen of Oare, as they now realised. Their victims were ill-prepared, but they were resourceful. Reaching the harbour, Eored saw that a battle raged by the waterfront. The quick-thinking fishermen had entangled the enemy in netting and as they fought in vain to free themselves from the mesh, they used whatever weapon, be it a rock or piece of metal, that came to hand to slay the captive. Eored watched one man underestimate his tangled foe, who, despite the mesh, managed to impale a dagger into the fisher's groin. Eored sprang forward and delivered a mighty axe blow to the raider's skull. There was nothing he could do for the fisherman, whose bloody hands clutched at a wound that was pouring forth his lifeblood.

Eored turned with seconds to spare, to see a Viking, sword and shield raised, running towards him. A chilling war cry from the advancing Norseman snapped the wheelwright from stunned immobility. He feared jamming his axe into the wooden shield, leaving himself vulnerable. Although not trained as a warrior, he employed what many a Saxon before him had used: guile. He dropped to one knee and swept the axe like a scythe, chopping into the leg of the onrushing Viking. The heavy steel blade sliced through the sinew and the Viking fell to the ground. Eored, already on his feet, crashed down the axe, cutting through the leather helm, metal rivets and all, to kill the invader in an instant.

Panting, Eored gazed around and, to his delight, understood that the Saxon townsfolk had prevailed. Alone, he had accounted for three, thus ungenerously including Cyneflaed's victim, but she would set him straight on that score later!

As for Deormund and Sibert's other men, they had to pass Oare first to reach Faversham. So, they saw smoke pouring from the small fishing settlement and watched the surviving Norse crewmen row out of the Creek before dropping the sail to speed away.

Panic squeezing his stomach in a vice-like grip, Deormund raced towards his brother's house, which he saw, to his relief, was spared from the Viking torches. To his horror, he saw the corpses of two Vikings in front of the threshold. A stitch in his side, and his lungs panting like a driven horse's, he burst into the building to find three faces grinning at his anxious countenance.

"What kept you, husband?"

"Are you all right?" His eyes swept from one to the other, noting that only Saewynn was not spattered with blood. The whole story came out, with Eored and Cyneflaed arguing over who was responsible for one of the bodies in the street.

In a daze, barely registering their words or their absurd argument, he reflected. Less than two years ago, he had lived his perfect life. Now, in the depths of his misery, Deormund recognized it for what it was: an ideal that gave him the attitude, the possibility, and the freedom to do what he had to do despite everything. He could scarcely believe that in such a short time the Norsemen, who, in his ignorance then, did not exist for him, had become a living nightmare in the broad light of day.

TWELVE
LYMINGE, KENT
800 AD

THEGN SIBERT HAD DECIDED TO RETURN TO LYMINGE anyway, to finish the work of levelling the ring fortification the Vikings had thrown up. So he was not inconvenienced when a messenger arrived from the Archdeacon of Christ Church, Canterbury, demanding that he meet him there.

"It seems we have a mystery to solve," Sibert announced gravely. "Archdeacon Wulfred informs me that the prioress of Lyminge Abbey has disappeared without a trace." The thegn frowned and shook his head. "It appears she was out of the confines for reasons of... as he puts it... *pastoral care*. She did not return as usual to fulfil her duties. The archdeacon has summoned the shire reeve but requires our help to search the area around Lyminge."

Deormund rode out with the thegn and fifteen other men, their horses' hoofs thundering on the old road to the east coast. On the outskirts of Lyminge, they spotted a group of four horsemen awaiting them; among them, a white steed stood out, partly for its colouring, but also its majestic bearing.

Thegn Sibert commented on it as soon as they drew up to the archdeacon and his party.

"Good day to you, Archdeacon Wulfred. What a fine beast you ride, if I might say so."

"Indeed, more than a horse to me, Thegn. I would say that Snawlic is a life companion, aren't you, fellow?" He patted the cheek of the steed and was rewarded with a gentle whinny.

"Snawlic. What an appropriate name! If ever a creature resembled a snowdrift, it is he," the thegn said and laughed.

Deormund smiled. In truth, he had never seen a finer horse. But they were not at Lyminge to admire horses, as the bluff shire reeve reminded them.

"My inquiries have drawn a blank. Nobody has seen her, nobody heard from her: it's as if Prioress Irmgard vanished into thin air."

"We should split up into groups of three to cover as much ground as possible," Sibert said. "First, we'll visit every corner of Lyminge. After that, if we make no progress, we'll start on the surrounding countryside. You three go down to the shore, ride down to the cliffs, check the caves." Likewise, he ordered the other groups to search in chosen directions until only he, the archdeacon and Deormund remained.

"We'll head towards the harbour," Sibert said. "The docks area is always full of dubious characters. I wouldn't want the prioress to have fallen into the wrong hands. That's why I've brought Deormund—in case of trouble. Our gentle deer herder is a street fighter," he guffawed.

Embarrassed, Deormund gazed at the archdeacon from under his lowered brow, but the prelate gave him a reassuring smile. The conversation between the two dignitaries was political and did not concern Deormund, who made it his business to halt at a roadside tavern to inquire about the prioress.

The white horse and the thegn's chestnut waited obediently for his return. The impatient riders said, "Well?" in unison, but Deormund shook his head. "The landlord knows nothing about a prioress and swears that none of his regulars would, either."

The archdeacon commended him on his thoroughness and they rode on until they entered Lyminge proper. There, Deormund's questioning brought no progress. Traders, stallholders, craftsmen and idlers alike denied all knowledge of the missing woman.

Time passed slowly while their queries drew puzzled expressions and much head-shaking. At last, they came to the docks area, where they visited a tavern, not just for duty, but to refresh their parched throats. The innkeeper, an agreeable fellow eager to please, suggested the ships in the harbour as a line of inquiry.

"See, Lord, there are a couple of traders tied up and they are full of strangers. Don't speak our language, and look!" His voice lowered and his head tilted to indicate a table in the dim far corner of the room. Deormund started at the sight of four Vikings drinking ale. "Tough, swaggering men, them are!" the landlord continued, "I heard tell them deal in slaves. I'm not making accusations, Lord, but them might have yon nun!"

"We'll take a look at their ship," Sibert said, quaffing his ale. "Those Norsemen won't be going anywhere in a hurry, by the look of them."

Their obliging landlord accompanied them to the door and pointed down to the harbour, indicating the vessel in question. It was not a longship like the ones Deormund had seen before, but a craft with higher sides and a broader beam. Unhitching their horses, they mounted and trotted them towards the wharf where the ship was moored. As they approached, they noticed movement aboard, so not all the crew was out enjoying the town's facilities.

Nearing the vessel, they saw a row of people chained together. At the sight of the three riders, two became agitated and, to silence them, received a flogging from a sturdy man wearing animal fur across his shoulders. Deormund discerned that the captives were both men and women. His heart pitied them; these people had lost their freedom and would be sold, according to the landlord, as slaves to Arabs. They would finish in the hands of those of another faith.

As he gazed, he noticed a woman staring more intently at them than the others. They were now level with the ship—a knar, although Deormund did not know the vessel classification —about fifty feet long and fifteen wide. The construction of overlapping oak planks was clear to him, but how many crewmen were still onboard was uncertain.

Suddenly, the staring woman burst into song, her voice sweet and lilting: *"God is our refuge and strength, an ever-present help in trouble. Therefore, we will not fear, though the earth give way and the mountains fall into the heart of the sea, though its waters roar and foam and the mountains quake with their surging."*

The archdeacon leapt off his horse and, agitated, cried to Sibert, "Psalm Forty-Six! She's the prioress, begging for deliverance. We must save her!"

Before either Sibert or Deormund could react, the prelate jumped aboard the Viking vessel, only to be caught by the rough hands of two Viking crewmen. Unceremoniously, they half-dragged him towards the tall man in the fur whom they had seen whip the captives earlier. He must be their leader, Deormund reasoned. Following Sibert's example, he tethered his horse beside the other two and stepped down carefully onto the gunwales of the cargo ship. His hand remained on the hilt of his sword as the taller man and the archdeacon haggled, each pointing in turn at the strained face of the captive nun, her head now bowed, her prayer ringing out amid her tears.

Not that he heard the details, but Deormund understood that the Viking was refusing the silver coins the archdeacon offered. He began to scan the vessel for crewmen should it come to a fight. How many? He counted five and saw one hand an axe to a comrade: a gesture that set his nerves jangling. On board, he calculated, there were six burly Vikings, so they were outnumbered. There were four others in the tavern and maybe more nearby. Combat might not be the best solution.

What was happening? The Viking spat into his hand and proffered it to the archdeacon, who did likewise. They had reached an agreement. The tall chieftain called to two crewmen who hurried to his side. Quick instructions led to them releasing the iron band and chain around the prioress's neck. Her hands were unbound before they helped her to stand.

What happened next amazed Deormund. They climbed back onto the quay, followed by three Vikings. Deormund assisted the nun by lifting her to the paving, to receive a grateful smile from her otherwise harrowed and tear-stained face. The archdeacon's sacrifice became apparent as the Vikings untethered the white horse and urged it towards the ship, where others prepared gangplanks to coax the beast into the belly of the ship. That was the price to make the Viking leader accede to the release of the nun. The deer herder understood the extent of the forfeit. He thought of Mistig, safely at Eored's home; he would not exchange the dog for anything or anyone.

Attempting to imagine the effect on the archdeacon of renouncing his Snawlic, he sidled close to the prelate and whispered, "We should gather our other men to fight these Norsemen, release the other prisoners and win back your horse."

"Nay, Deormund, you have a good heart. But see yonder ship? It is another Viking trader. Do you think they would stand by? I'm afraid we would pay a far higher price than a steed. I will buy another. It won't be Snawlic," he said sorrowfully. "But come, help the prioress mount your horse. We two will walk together to the abbey, my son." The archdeacon steadfastly kept his eyes averted, refusing to watch his beloved steed being manhandled aboard the Norse cargo ship.

The prioress, however, never took her eyes off the vessel that would have borne her to Constantinople and some dreadful fate. Her lips moved in silent prayer. Gratefully, she allowed Deormund to lift her onto his horse. As he did so, he noticed the noble structure of her countenance. This was no ceorl's daughter but a noblewoman, destined to be a slave had they not intervened. In equal measure, the deer herder felt exultant and dismayed. Their efforts had liberated the prioress but the other captives, less prominent members of society, were doomed to maltreatment somewhere he had never heard of. He turned to Thegn Sibert, riding beside the nun.

"Is there nought we can do for the other prisoners, Thegn?"

The thegn shook his head.

"You cannot end the slave trade with your sword, Deormund. We must do what we can to prevent others of our Kentish folk from falling into Viking hands. That is the task we are about at present. The prioress is an exceptional case. I'm afraid the captives will have to hope they fall into decent hands."

"I will pray for them," the nun said.

It was all Deormund could manage to refrain from snorting in disgust. Rapidly, a hatred of the Vikings was building up in his bosom. On their way to Lyminge Abbey, they encountered some of their comrades. The thegn sent them away to round up the others. They would meet in the afternoon at the earthworks of the previous day. Meanwhile, Prioress Irmgard promised them a meal in the refectory; it was, she said, the least she could do to repay their kindness.

After their lunch, levelling the Viking ring fortress was a sapping business. Used to enclosures, Deormund calculated that the circular stronghold had a diameter of around a hundred and twenty-two yards, but without pacing it, he could not be sure. With the rampart, he did pace out the width, measuring it at forty-two feet quite accurately. The ramparts had four breaks at regular opposed intervals for gates. They had to level the earthen ramparts to the ground, which meant blistered hands for him and his comrades, but removing them would render the intended fortress useless to any raiders. Fortunately, it was the only one of its kind they had found in the area.

"Come on, men! It will be dark in a couple of hours. I want to see some progress today!" bellowed Thegn Sibert, setting an example by flinging a shovelful of earth into the ditch at the foot of the rampart. Deormund redoubled his efforts, as did the men on either side of him, but they knew that to arrive at ground level all around the circuit would take many days. *Damn the Vikings!* Deormund thought, muttering horrible curses that made the man next to him laugh.

"Thegn," the deer herder called, "tomorrow, we should enlist the townsfolk to dig. After all, this toiling is for their safety.

"Ay, well said!"

"Good idea!" others joined in.

The thegn said nothing but must have reflected on the suggestion, for the next morning, the shire reeve arrived with an armed escort and twenty men, their hands bound.

"Thegn Sibert! Here's the score of miscreants I promised you. I've emptied the gaol. They can gain their liberty with a couple of days of willing work. Any slackers will face my wrath and can forget about freedom! Those who put their backs into honest toil will go free, clear?"

The hope and eagerness in the prisoners' faces spoke volumes about their decision. So, with more hard workers, within three days the Viking fortress no longer existed other than as a brown circle. That, too, would soon grass over, as Deorman told anyone disposed to listen.

In the continued absence of Aethelhard, Archbishop of Canterbury, Archdeacon Wulfred commanded proceedings. If Deormund thought that demolishing the ring fortress was the end of their engineering activities, he was sorely mistaken as they were just beginning. As Sibert pointed out, one aspect was preventing the Vikings from setting up an encampment; "... the other, friend Deormund, is to prevent them entering our burhs or attacking our monasteries."

Thus, the next job was to reinforce or repair the defensive walls wherever required. That work kept them occupied in Lyminge before they moved on to Reculver. There, the monastery of St Mary needed protection. Once that was done, towards the end of the year, to Deormund's delight, the thegn revealed his plans for the new year. They would go to Sceapig, where the monastery at Minster sought attention. This meant that soon they would return to Faversham, where he would be reunited with Cyneflaed. Then, after the festivities for the birth of the Lord, they would transfer to Sceapig.

Deormund was delighted when the thegn told him, "Your wife can come, too. She can stay with your parents and you, my friend, will supply us with fresh venison."

THIRTEEN
FAVERSHAM, KENT
801 AD

AFTER THE FESTIVITIES FOR THE BIRTH OF THE LORD, THE New Year brought confusion and danger. First, Archdeacon Wulfred arrived in the thegn's hall, bearing a letter from Alcuin in the Frankish court. His agitation prevented him from giving a coherent explanation of his worries but the following day, Thegn Sibert summoned other nobles of the area to a council meeting with the prelate. Deormund and his closest comrades were present in their role as bodyguards to the thegn.

Sibert began the consultation with a brief introduction:

"My lords, friends, welcome. We are gathered here in the name of the Lord and our king, Coenwulf, to hear the words of Archdeacon Wulfred, who bears tidings from overseas. We must hear him and take whatever action is necessary. Without further ado, I invite you, Archdeacon, to take the floor."

The archdeacon, pallid and concerned, stood before them. His strained visage bestowed an air of gravitas on the proceedings before he had even uttered a word. Although the attention of the assembly was already riveted on him, with an unnecessary flourish, the prelate produced a document from his robe.

"This letter comes to me, written in scholarly hand, from the court of Emperor Charles in Frankia." He paused to stare around the hall as if to verify that each person had understood the importance of its provenance. "The sender is a scholar well known to me and of impeccable reputation, born and raised in Northumbria. As you will know,"—Deormund did not— "that kingdom has suffered turmoil of late, with nobles conspiring to assassinate King Æthelred five years ago. As you all know,"— again, news to Deormund— "he was succeeded by Osbald, whose reign lasted only twenty-seven days before he was deposed. Eardwulf became king in May of that year."

Judging by the heads put together and low murmuring all around him, the shrugging of shoulders and head-shaking, the deer herder concluded that the gathering was no wiser than he about Northumbrian matters.

The archdeacon clicked his tongue impatiently and raised the letter above his head to recapture attention.

"My correspondent informs me that the emperor of the Franks is infuriated by this state of affairs. Emperor Charles, he tells me, began a long invective against men who rebel, calling them traitors, murderers of lords, and men worse than heathens. Having given his protection to King Eardwulf, and hearing that our King Coenwulf has granted asylum to other claimants to the throne of Northumbria, he has lent his support to Eardwulf's proposed invasion of Mercia."

The uproar in the hall made further speech impossible, so the archdeacon, his face sour, pinched and paler than ever, sank into the seat provided for him. Thegn Sibert, tense and annoyed, rapped the hilt of his seax on the table and bellowed a command for order. At last, silence returned and the prelate rose again. He cleared his throat and continued.

"The men of Kent must take up arms in defence of our overlord Coenwulf." More head-shaking and growls of dissent greeted these words. "As yet, the king has not mustered the Kentish fyrd. It is only a matter of time, for my informants assure me that Eardwulf is even now raising an army and planning to march south."

Thegn Sibert gazed around the room whilst indicating the archdeacon's seat, gesturing him to sit. Taking charge of the proceedings, he declared firmly, "We must prepare for war with Northumberland. Go your separate ways, but be ready to respond to a call to arms. I will send messengers as soon as I receive news from Mercia."

The thegn was instantly surrounded by other noblemen, each wishing to express his opinion. Deormund turned to his former assailant, now his trusted comrade, Eadlac.

"From what they say, it seems that we'll be marching off to war shortly."

Eadlac frowned, touched the hilt of his sword and grinned. The burly bodyguard glanced towards Sibert. "I might need this sooner than that to free our thegn from his angry friends!"

Deormund looked in the same direction; sure enough, as he stared, a finger jabbed the thegn's chest and a bristling red face thrust close to Sibert's.

"Let's move in, Eadlac!"

Deormund stepped towards his lord, pulling and thrusting men aside to reach him. The hefty bodyguard behind him ensured that the protests at his forceful passage did not become physical. Reaching Thegn Sibert's side, the deer herder placed the flat of his hand on the furious nobleman's chest and pushed him away. The enraged and now offended man reached for his sword, but Deormund's was already out, the point pressing against the other man's throat.

"Enough," thundered Sibert, "lest our meeting end in bloodshed! Deormund, sheath your weapon!"

The deer herder-cum-bodyguard glared at the furious

visage of Sibert's interlocutor. The man seemed deflated, so Deormund made a show of sheathing his sword. Could it be that the nobleman was rightly angered at having to prepare for war on behalf of a king across the border from Kent? After all, whilst he had led a quiet life on Sceapig, he had known nothing about Mercia and its kings. But now, he realised, there were dangers everywhere while a man needed a strong lord for protection. Whatever happened, he would serve Sibert faithfully even if it meant, as seemed likely, going to war.

Not all the lords surrounding Sibert were as hostile as the one who had been at the point of Deormund's sword. Mixed feelings coursed through the hall, causing outbreaks of arguing and discussions; only when the building emptied did the bodyguards relax, to ask themselves, and each other, whether a war was in the offing. Overhearing them, Sibert spoke grimly.

"Listen, men, I believe that we must cross the estuary into the territory of the East Saxons within a few days. War is the last thing I want, but if the king commands, we must obey or face the consequences."

Three days later, a messenger arrived from the royal palace of Tamworth where King Coenwulf resided. Sibert reacted at once, sending his riders out to convoke the Kentish lords with their warriors to Faversham. Two more days passed before an army assembled in the town. Sibert ordered Deormund to carry his emblem: a triangular device, bearing three golden lions on a red background, attached to the end of a long pole. This was a dubious honour that would focus enemy attention on him in battle. For the moment, he trotted his horse proudly beside his lord, at the head of the thegn's men as they marched to the ford across the Thames.

Wulfred, the scion of a noble family of the Middle Saxons, rode in the party beside Bishop Waermund of Rochester. On the journey, Deormund had no idea how important their presence and the accompaniment of other clerics would prove during the following days. Reacting to the news that Northumbrian troops had invaded Mercia and were heading towards Tamworth, King Coenwulf marched eastwards to join forces with the Kentish fyrd.

The Kentish encampment, campfire flames casting a flickering glow over the warriors' faces, tripled in extension with the new arrivals. Deormund strolled over to watch the Mercians pitch their tents and light their fires. Never had he seen so many men gathered in one place. This thought brought his stroll to a halt. Would not the Northumbrians have the same number of warriors, or more? The full horror of the imminent battle struck him at that moment. With his ignorance of politics, he could not suspect that the headcount might alter the course of events. Like a high tide ebbing with the pull of the moon, the allegiance of the East Angles drew back the waves of war. King Coenwulf, unknown to his enemy, Eardwulf, had declared overlordship of that kingdom, which had submitted to him. Apprised of that fact and warned that Coenwulf might be prepared to engage in peace talks, the King of Northumbria opened negotiations. The first Deormund learnt of this was when Thegn Sibert ordered him to fetch the standard he had planted in front of the thegn's tent.

"Get your horse, Deormund and bring my banner, for we ride to meet the Northumbrians."

———

THE TWO KINGS met on equal terms, each adding bishops and nobles to the parley. Deormund stood guard over his thegn and his presence, along with others like him, guaranteed that no treachery would be perpetrated by either side. In a position to hear every proposal and counter-suggestion, he was able to recount what took place at the fateful meeting to his comrades as they drank ale around their fire that evening.

"It's going to be peace, my friends. Ay," he reassured the incredulous faces of his companions, keyed-up as they were on what they supposed was the eve of battle, "we will not fight on the morrow, but return to our homes."

"How can you be so sure, Deormund?" the deep voice of Eadlac rumbled.

"Because I was standing next to Thegn Sibert all the time. Our thegn is a fine speaker but, in truth, the archdeacon and his friend, the bishop of Rochester, swung the talks towards peace. It seems that the emperor of the Franks likes to interfere in Angle-land," he lowered his voice and added in a mysterious tone, made more intriguing by the flickering ruddy light of the fire, "aye, there's more to all this than meets the eye."

"What do you mean?" asked Wardric, his old sword tutor.

"It seems that the Franks are under pressure from heathen foes and that Emperor Charles wishes for the stability Christians provide across the Channel. That is why he has pledged his support to King Eardwulf and why the bishops were so important in the parley. There was a lot of talk about Christians fighting each other whilst pagans look on with glee, waiting only for the opportunity to pounce when true believers are weakened."

"There's some sense in that," Eadlac's voice rumbled from deep in his chest.

"King Coenwulf's power has grown, but he had to agree to expel Eardwulf's rivals from his kingdom. That's when I thought the peace talks would break down, because he refused to hand them to the Northumbrians."

"Eardwulf would kill them. He showed no mercy when he took the throne." Wardric seemed well-informed on political matters. "So, what happened?"

"Oh, he consented to expel them to Wales. That settled it. The Northumbrians agreed to that and to withdraw at once from Mercia. Eardwulf had to respect Coenwulf's overlordship of East Anglia as part of the agreement. He didn't seem very happy about it, I can tell you! Anyway, we all live to fight another day: peace, it is!"

On the ride to Kent, Deormund edged his horse closer in order to speak to Wardric.

"I've never fought in a battle, only in skirmishes," he admitted.

The veteran warrior curled his lip. "You sound disappointed, but instead, you want to thank the Lord, young fellow. If the talks had failed, there would have been a great slaughter. Maybe neither of us would be here," he glanced upwards, "to see that blue sky and those feathery white clouds," he said, in his deep Dorset burr. "Fear not, Deormund, your time to fight will come, likely sooner than you'd wish, what with you soon to be a father and all."

Deormund grinned; it seemed his forthcoming paternity was common knowledge, whereas he hadn't thought that Cyneflaed might have become a widow with a babe when he'd ridden off to war. But nothing would have happened to him, in any case, would it?

I hadn't thought of that!

He gazed around at the rolling countryside and the fast-flowing river with fresh eyes. A curlew called. Suddenly, being alive seemed to be a privilege he had not considered when he rode away from Faversham. The beauty around him made him think of Cyneflaed and her tearful face when riding away from the Rhegn's hall. He promised himself that he would not take life, and especially his wife, for granted again. For the hundredth time, he wondered whether the babe growing inside her would be a girl or a boy. He had no preference, except that the child be born healthy and the mother survive childbirth.

He thought of Bebbe and smiled broadly. His mother would be delighted with a fourth grandchild. For the first time, he hoped it would be a boy, not for himself, but for a grandmother who had only granddaughters.

FOURTEEN
FAVERSHAM, KENT
802 AD

WITH THE BIRTH OF A SON, CHOOSING A NAME THREW Deormund into confusion. For several hours, he considered calling the babe Hartman—a common enough name—inspired by his fondness for deer. Finally, his good sense and love of his father won the tussle. So, little *Asculf* kicked and gurgled happily in the cot Deormund had made on his return from the confrontation with the Northumbrians.

Not long ago, on Sceapig, he had considered his life perfect, but now, living with his comely wife and cradling his son in his arms, he rarely missed his former existence. However, it so often happens that, just when a man considers his circumstances ideal, life rears up and kicks him in the ribs harder than an angered mule. The panicking Prioress Irmgard, on behalf of Lyminge Abbey, arrived at the thegn's hall three weeks before Easter and Deormund's domestic idyll was instantly over.

"The Norsemen are back!" she cried. "Abbess Selethrytha begs succour! The nuns are in danger. Please come to our aid!"

Thegn Sibert did not hesitate, but gathered his men and called upon the neighbouring lords. Within hours, he rode out, banner streaming, at the head of three-score warriors. Deormund, as before, bore the standard and dwelt on how different was his state of mind this time. Little Asculf needed to grow up under his father's loving tutelage and, he thought, *Cyneflaed will be bereft if anything happens to me.*

"Cheer up, Deormund! You wanted to test your battle skills, didn't you? Now's your chance, my friend."

"I was thinking about my family, Eadlac."

"That's the worst thing you can do! Don't fret! I'll watch your back."

"And I, yours!"

They rode on the few miles to Lyminge in companionable conversation, debating whether their repairs to the abbey's defensive wall would withhold a Viking assault or if indeed they had already succumbed. The latter did not bear thinking about. The fortune of having a dry spell before Easter, making the road to Lyminge easy to travel, was offset by the distance of seven leagues. The willing pace of men marching behind them meant that they would arrive within two hours. As Eadlac pointed out, in that time, much could change.

"Especially if you add the hour it took the prioress to gallop from Lyminge," Deormund added gloomily.

"I must ask her how she slipped past the Viking lookouts. We could use her skills," Eadlac said, only half-jokingly.

They could smell the salt air as they approached Lyminge, but from the approach road, they could not see the sea. It was therefore impossible to know whether there was a lone longship or more pulled onto the beach. Would they be outnumbered? Surely, their force could cope with the crew of one longship, but what if there were two or more crews?

Had the Saxons known that the Norsemen's tactic was to sail a solitary ship near a temptingly soft target to seize silver and provisions in a hit-and-run raid, they would have felt more relaxed. The Vikings, informed of the arriving Kentish force, were uncowed, as the aim of each Norseman was to destroy his enemy or die in the attempt. A glorious death guaranteed access to Valhalla on the wings of the Valkyrie: entry to the Feasting Hall of the gods.

The first sign of the Viking presence, on the level ground facing the abbey, was the sound of weapons beating rhythmically on their shields. When the new arrivals drew into view, two hundred yards from the colourful compact line of circular shields, a mighty roar like that of a wounded beast greeted them. Quickly, the Saxon riders dismounted whilst Thegn Sibert organised his warriors into three lines. Each man had brought a javelin, so they advanced cautiously, awaiting the command to hurl them at the enemy.

They closed to within twenty-five yards, half-expecting the Vikings to rush them in a surprise attack. They were wrong; the disciplined foe waited calmly for the expected fall of darts. A shouted order came, to release a dense hail of javelins on the Norsemen. Their shields parried most of the sharp points but such was the intensity of the launched weapons that half a dozen Vikings were killed or wounded. The Men of Kent charged forward, their axes or shield bosses battering against the wooden wall.

Deorman had planted the standard near the horses so that his hands were free to fight. When he approached the seemingly impenetrable wall, he had a momentary glimpse of a head and shoulders through a chink between shields. Knowing it might be his only chance, heedless of his safety, he lunged and swung his sword. It was the slightest opportunity that might, or might not, succeed in equal measure. Good fortune assisted and rewarded his temerity; a swift flash of his scrupulously-honed blade brought a scream from behind the shield. The Viking holding it collapsed to the ground, enabling Deormund and Eadlac to leap through the gap. He jumped onto the shield covering the dead man's chest, using it as a support to spin around, noticing in an instant the gaping slash he had inflicted to the throat of his victim.

The giant figure of Eadlac lurched past him, brushing his arm as he turned and, in seconds, the two of them were again shoulder to shoulder, hacking into the exposed backs of the Norsemen defending their line. Once a shield-wall is broken, it is no longer useful as a defensive barrier. Thanks to Deormund and Eadlac, more Kentish warriors poured through the gap, swinging the tide of battle in their favour, the Norse resistance now almost at an end. Terrible minutes of slaughter against an enemy in numerical inferiority followed; the Vikings, now deprived of their trusted defensive line, succumbed until not one remained alive. At last, after the deafening sounds of battle, the mews of the wheeling gulls and the whisper of the sea breeze in their ears came as a gentle balm.

Deormund and Eadlac embraced and laughed in each other's face, promising wild celebrations with the reckless consumption of strong ale. The warrior-deer herder, exultant, suddenly remembered the thegn's words from many weeks before. *Give me a chance and I'll burn their ship, too.* Leaving Eadlac gaping in surprise, he staggered over to the thegn, his energy drained from the herculean effort expended in battle. "Lord, a word if you will!"

"Deormund, I know it was you who broke through the Norse lines and I will recompense you as befits."

"It's not that which I'm after, Thegn, but I beg you to remember what you told me months ago." He repeated the words.

"By all the saints, you are right! First, we must bury our dead and then burn the Viking corpses. My man tells me we lost seven of our comrades."

"Ay, Lord, but we killed the whole crew of the pirate ship."

"Thanks be to God!"

An idea came to Deormund. "Lord, we should burn the Norsemen in their ship so that we rid ourselves of both at once in the easiest way."

The thegn stared hard at the deer herder. "Combat inspires you, Deormund. I will give the orders."

Vikings did not sail without a cask of pitch onboard to make torches. When pillaging, they flung flaming brands to burn houses and induce terror. Deormund sniffed out the barrel of the black substance after inspecting the deserted vessel. They found and removed sacks of plundered treasure that included precious crosses robbed from unfortunate churches located who-knew-where, gold and silver coins, and cured meat. All these they unloaded onto the beach, whence they dragged the Viking corpses and laid them respectfully in the belly of their ship. Deormund had unwittingly assumed command by issuing orders. The thegn's men, respectful of his valour in the earlier battle, sprang to obey whilst a curious smile twitched on his lord's lips, but Sibert left him to it.

They smeared pitch on the Norsemen's clothing, over the wooden surfaces of the vessel and, making good their retreat, flung five blazing torches, also prepared with pitch, which instantly produced flames that soared high around the towering mast. Willing shoulders heaved the longship from the sand to the sea and, with one last enormous effort, they shoved the infernal vessel into the water. The crackling and snapping flames sent dense smoke pouring over the waves as the longship floated away on the receding tide. The exhausted men turned around in surprise, to behold the strange sight of cheering, clapping nuns standing at the high-water line of the strand! In front of the nuns stood Prioress Irmgard, her arm linked through that of Abbess Selethrytha.

The two women smiled sweetly at the men by the water's edge.

"Look, Deormund, another shield-wall!" Eadlac joked. "They've forgotten their shields. We should charge them!"

"I've told you, find yourself a betrothed and you'll stop acting like one of those..." he turned to point at the longship. His mouth fell open as he stared at the now-distant craft, fire spectacularly devouring the mast so that it began to lean at a curious angle before dropping in an arc of flames and sparks; suddenly, the blazing furled sail extinguished in the seawater. "One of those Vikings," he ended with a grin. "Attack the nuns and you'll likely meet the same end."

"They don't look ferocious to me, come on!"

They followed the thegn and the others up the beach to greet the grateful nuns. Deormund arrived in time to catch the Abbess mid-sentence: "...even so, Thegn, I shall write to the Archbishop. We can no longer remain exposed here in Lyminge. I have to think about my women and, not least, the sacred relics of Saint Ethelburga, our foundress. Our abbey is far too close to the shore. I will beg for premises in the city of Canterbury. Only by God's grace did you arrive in time to deliver us this day. Another time, we may not be so fortunate." She turned an anguished face to her prioress as if in search of confirmation.

"You should talk to Archdeacon Wulfred, Mother. He is in charge of defences in Kent. I believe your supplication will be well received as it is within his remit," said Thegn Sibert.

Deormund nodded as if involved in the conversation; he had heard Wulfred speak at the parley in the land of the East Saxons. If anyone could organise a new abbey in Canterbury for Abbess Selethrytha, it was the competent prelate. The deer herder glanced out to sea, but there was no sign of the destroyed longship—it had likely gone under, taking the dead Vikings to the bottom.

"We should bury your valiant warriors in our graveyard and give them a Christian Mass," the abbess said gently.

Arrangements made for the solemn requiem, Deormund, Eadlac and a small number of like-minded companions postponed all thoughts of revelry, instead, sorrowfully praying for the souls of their fallen comrades. Any wild celebrations would have to wait until their return to Faversham. After the burial, speaking directly to Deormund, the thegn said, "Two or three days in Faversham and then we are on our way to Sceapig. So, don't get too drunk, my lad, because you'll be taking your family with you, I suppose."

The euphoria of victory now a thing of the past, Deormund had no trouble behaving with moderation. The comfortable companionship of a select group of Sibert's guards allowed him to explain his modest consumption.

"Heed me, friends, a man is fortunate when surrounded by a loving family and must not abuse his luck. Tomorrow, we cross to Sceapig; the isle is in my blood, my reputation is there in the safekeeping of my parents. I will not arrive there with bloodshot eyes and slurred speech like you ne'er-do-wells!"

This short discourse brought much laughter and ribaldry, back-slapping and jesting, but was accepted with good grace. Deormund was able to sit back and tell his interested companions what they would find on Sceapig. Mostly, they were curious about the monastery at Minster, for their task would be to reinforce its defences.

"It's nearly as old as the abbey at Lyminge. When I was a boy, my grandfather told me that his grandsire's father saw it built in the reign of King Ecgberht, who gave the land to his mother—Seaxburh of Ely."

"Where's Ely?" Eadlac asked.

"In the kingdom of the East Angles." Wardric was always the most informed and interested of the deer herder's companions. "But look here," the veteran added, "if what Deormund says is right, the monastery must be well over a hundred years old."

"Nearer one hundred and fifty," Deormund assured him. "I reckon it will need strengthening. The abbey is exposed to the wind and salty air. I haven't been there in years but remember the walls being of a soft yellowish stone. You heard Abbess Selethrytha yesterday, she complained of being too near the sea; well, Minster is nearer and there's a beach below for easy landing. Luckily, the abbey is on higher ground but that wouldn't save it from a determined assault, especially in its present state."

"You care, don't you, Deormund? Do you have family in the monastery, by chance?" Wardric asked.

"There's a cousin, Beonna, who took the veil."

"Beonna, eh? That's a pretty name. I'll wager she's just as fair," Eadlac said and chuckled.

Deormund glowered at him. "I told you yesterday, you're no better than a Norseman! Find yourself a bride, big lump, before you end up skewered! Oh, by the way, talking of spitted meat—I promise you the best roast venison you've ever eaten."

FIFTEEN
SCEAPIG, KENT
802 AD

"You know the island like the back of your hand, Deormund, so I'm putting you in charge of the men while you're on Sceapig. I'll send Wardric with you in case you need a wise old head. I'm going to Canterbury to consult with Archdeacon Wulfred."

"I won't let you down, Thegn."

Sibert knew that, for he had noticed the deer herder's leadership abilities. His journey to Canterbury was also based on this observation, but he was too canny to anticipate his plans to Deormund, lest they went awry.

As the religious house at Minster was a nunnery, Deormund knew little about his new responsibility. He gained access to the abbey with the excuse of visiting his cousin Beonna. They had not spoken for the three years since she had finished her novitiate. Eyeing her relative with suspicion, she asked, "What is the true reason for your visit, Deormund?"

"It is correct that I wished to see you, cousin and I confess that I have an underlying motive." He tried his most disarming smile, the one that achieved results with Cyneflaed.

Beonna flushed and lowered her head for an instant but when she raised it, there was a flash of anger in her eyes. "You had better tell me what it is you want of me. Make it good, otherwise this conversation is over."

"I'm sorry. I did not mean to offend."

He went on to explain the task entrusted to him and his men, ending gently, "So, you see, Beonna, it is a delicate matter. I wish to bring a score of warriors into a female sanctuary to do the work. I seek your help to learn what kind of person I will be dealing with in the abbess. Your counsel will be invaluable. I need to approach her in the right way. You know I am but a clumsy deer herder."

He watched her closely, noting the gleam in her eye when he asked for her cooperation but also the return of distrust at his false modesty.

"Our Mother Superior is a kind woman. Did not Abbess Irma allow you to visit your cousin? I feel sure that my counsel is unnecessary, Deormund. I remember you as a respectful youth. Your approach to the abbess need only be reverential. After all, you and your men come in her best interests."

"I do not wish to frighten you, Beonna, but the Norsemen are pagans who worship false gods, detesting our religion. They show no mercy, not even to children and babes. Our task is to make your abbey less vulnerable."

"This you must tell our Superior."

His keen eye did not miss how her right hand twisted the pale-green cloth of her dress in anxiety.

"Beonna, can you arrange for me to meet the abbess?"

"I-I think so. Wait here by the well. I must speak with Prioress Leowen. She will know what to do."

Deormund settled on the yellow stonework of the well. Seated there, he contemplated the building material. Running his hand over it, he noted its smooth texture. Knowing nothing about rock formation, he could not be sure of its properties. Casting a furtive glance around the courtyard, assuring himself that his presence was largely unnoticed by the nuns going about their daily chores, he pulled his seax from his belt and, shielding his action as best he could, he scratched at the well stone with the point. The tip of the blade gouged into the friable rock, leaving a furrow several inches long.

"Deormund!"

He started; the angry face of his cousin mirrored that of a middle-aged nun standing next to her.

"Why are you damaging our well?" Beonna's accusatory tone was justified. He hadn't meant to score so deeply.

"I beg your forgiveness. I was testing the resistance of this stone." He thrust his seax back into its sheath. "It is the same rock that sustains the gates. I'm sorry. I should have waited for your reply."

"Abbess Irma will receive you; come with me, I am her prioress," the other nun said.

Although her tone was severe, there was no hardness in the reassuring grey eyes of the nun. Deormund, feeling hopeful, jumped up to follow her but, as he was turning away, he looked back and saw Beonna running her fingers over the groove he had created as if to heal it with her delicate touch.

Abbess Irma greeted him with cool politeness, listening to his words with an increasingly troubled face. For her age, which was betrayed by the iron-grey hair that rebelled against her wimple, she had the skin of a much younger woman, with no wrinkles or sagging. Even so, his warning had brought an anxious frown to her countenance.

"Is this danger you speak of imminent, Deormund?"

"Mother, we cannot be certain, but the sea is infested with these Norse pirates. Increasingly, there are raids on targets that are easy for them to overwhelm." He tried to judge the effect of his words. How much did he need to frighten her? How much to convince her? Reaching an interior compromise, he told her of Abbess Selethrytha's request to move her charges from Lyminge to Canterbury. "I should mention that the abbey at Lyminge is farther from the sea than yours, Abbess."

"Is fighting them the only solution, my son? Can we not negotiate should they reach our gates?"

The deer herder looked pityingly at the holy woman; she had no idea of the nature of the sea wolves.

"Mother, you do not know the temper of the heathen. They are not to be trusted. They glory in deceiving their enemy, almost as much as slaying them. I have seen what they do to women and children." He noticed her involuntary shudder. "Ay, I have fought them man to man. I can testify to their ferocity. That is why I am here today, seeking permission to bring men into the abbey grounds. We must use all means available to strengthen the defences of your convent."

"I will not tolerate any unseemliness. My sisters have chosen a life of seclusion and prayer to devote themselves to Christ."

"I will answer for my men's behaviour, Mother. They will work on the reinforcements and nought else! We will set up a camp outside the walls to retire to after the day's toil. With your permission, today I will bring the wisest among us to inspect the fortifications."

"Saint Seaxburh's is a nunnery, not a fortress, Deormund! Although I'll admit, our foundress of blessed memory did not have to defend against pirates two hundred years ago. I dare say you will find much labour for your poor men!"

"Lady—er, forgive me—Mother, it is the concern of Archdeacon Wulfred that we dedicate our minds and bodies to the task."

Having overcome her initial diffidence, and obtained

consent to proceed, Deormund brought Wardric to inspect the abbey defences. The veteran warrior studied the yellowish stone of the walls with a mixture of curiosity and perplexity.

"Want to know what I think?"

Deorman smiled at the pleasant accent he had grown so fond of. He clapped the Dorset man on the back and said, "Isn't that why I brought you here?"

The warrior chuckled. "I suppose. Anyway, back then, the abbess at the time was the daughter of the King of the East Angles, then, she married the King of Kent—"

"Thanks for the history lesson, Wardric, but what has that to do with this yellow stone?"

"Patience never was your strong point, Deormund. What I'm saying is that she was so important and rich that she could afford whatever her heart desired."

"So?"

The veteran's smile resembled a reproving sneer.

"So, my thought is that this stone isn't a local stone, or any other I've seen in this country. She probably had it brought over from Frankia. There's not enough rock on Sceapig to build a house, never mind a defensive wall."

"True, there are no quarries on Sceapig."

Wardric was not interested in his friend's opinion since he had already decided. Instead, rather like the deer herder previously, he scratched at the rock with his seax, then dug into the mortar between the blocks.

When he'd finished, the impatient younger man said, "Well?"

"It's not a hard rock, it's fair to say, but no pirate raiding party will strive to breach it when it's easier to attack the gate."

"What do you think we should do?"

"I say that we put all our efforts into strengthening the

entry, whilst also building two wooden towers on the ramparts at either side to ward off any possible assault."

"Splendid! It's not as great a task as I feared. We should start cutting down timber in the woods early tomorrow. We'll need oxen and a cart to transport it. I'll arrange that here in Elmley."

The willing band set to work in the forest the next morning, with careful, selective felling and trimming of the branches. Meanwhile, Deormund went home to explain his requirements to his father, who promised to convince a neighbour to provide oxen and a cart the next day.

When Deormund hastened towards the abbey gates, striding through the morning dew, he found a friendly, smiling face prepared to greet him from his perch on the cart. The oxen grazed stoically beside the cart, temporarily freed from the yoke that lay on the ground.

"I thought it best to unyoke them; otherwise, they get restless," the ceorl explained.

This simple loan of animals and equipment meant a lot to Deormund, but was just the start of cooperation that would surprise him to an extent that he could not have dreamt of at that moment.

The first inkling that his task might expand came after three weeks of unremitting toil. Already, one of the twin towers stood tall above the abbey gates when a messenger arrived for Deormund. After a few minutes of rapid consultation, the man returned to the ferry and his horse tethered on the other side of the Swale.

Deormund strode over to Wardric. "Old friend, I'm leaving you in charge. I have to ride to Canterbury at the thegn's order. It will keep me away three days."

"What does Thegn Sibert want?"

Deormund's brow creased. "I'm not sure. The messenger

said something about signing a charter. That can't be right. The dullard likely delivered a garbled message—whoever heard of a deer herder signing a charter? One thing is clear, though— Sibert requires my presence for some purpose. You'll need more timber for the second tower. Why don't you get the felling and hauling done while I'm away?"

"You might as well go now," said the veteran warrior, pulling his cloak tighter around him to ward off the spring wind that blasted chill from the sea and went howling around the new wooden tower and whistling through every slight gap in the sturdy timber gates. "That way, you'll get to play around with Cyneflaed." He nudged and winked at the herder. "Go on! You'll need more time with her. You can't travel now, anyway, it's too late in the day."

"You're right; it'll soon be dusk. I'll head off home to my wife and little warrior! Don't allow any slacking." He didn't doubt that the men would work as hard as ever because Wardric was the one who chivvied them, Deormund serving more as an off-the-scene authority figure whenever minor complaints arose.

After a night in the loving bosom of his family, Deormund set out at dawn for Canterbury, making a brief deviation to collect a horse from the thegn's stables. On horseback, he would arrive with daylight, whereas on foot, he would need an overnight stay. In truth, he wished to reach Canterbury as soon as possible because he hadn't understood the thegn's message, so curiosity plagued him. It seemed strange, though, that the appointment was at Christ Church cathedral.

Expecting to meet Thegn Sibert, his surprise at being greeted by Archdeacon Wulfred was instantly replaced by astonishment at the prelate's form of address.

"Well met, Thegn Deormund!"

The deer herder gasped; there must be some mistake. Had

he mistaken him for a thegn?

"Forgive me, Father, but you err. I am no thegn but a simple ceorl."

The countenance of the prelate clouded and in a cutting voice he declared, "Simple ceorls are not wont to correct their superiors, Thegn."

Was there a smile in those penetrating blue eyes?

"Again, I beg forgiveness, Archdeacon, but I am confused; you address me with a title that does not belong to me."

"Oh, but it does, Deormund!"

The voice of Thegn Sibert came from behind a column supporting the high roof of the cathedral. Deormund spun round. "Lord, I—"

"No longer call me Lord, Deormund, for we are equals in the eyes of God and the law."

"How can this be?"

The nobleman laughed, the sound reverberating around the sacred edifice.

"Hush!" reproved the Archdeacon, "This is the house of God! It is unseemly to raise the voice."

"Begging your pardon, Wulfred, but look at his face!" The thegn turned red with the effort to stifle another guffaw while tears formed in his eyes. "Did you not receive my message that you were to sign a charter raising you to thegn?"

"Lord—er, I mean Sibert—the messenger's brain must have been numbed by the cold wind, for he simply told me to come here."

Another chortle stifled, Sibert adopted a business-like tone. "I will speak with my envoy later, but now we must retire to sign the deeds."

Confused but at the same time excited, Deormund followed the two men in a daze as he struggled to come to terms with the meaning of these events.

The archdeacon led them into a small room furnished with a table and three chairs. They sat while the prelate took charge.

"First, let me explain, Deormund, for I see by your face that you are bewildered. Our thinking is this: Sceapig is part of our kingdom, but an area that largely belongs to the Church thanks to King Eorcenberht, who donated it to his Queen Seaxburh—"

"Ah, the saint of the abbey—" Deormund interrupted.

"Exactly!" The archdeacon gave him a sour look to discourage further interruptions. "Thus, the saintly queen bequeathed the land to the Church. In my role as vicar to the Archbishop of Canterbury, it is within my gift to endow these lands and the income deriving. Sceapig, owing to its location," the piercing blue eyes met his to see whether they found comprehension there, and satisfied, the prelate continued, "is particularly vulnerable to seaborne threat. Sibert tells me that even now you are in charge of strengthening the Abbey of St Seaxburh and that you have remarkable leadership qualities. What sense would it have, then, if you finish work on the abbey only to depart, leaving the rest of the island unprotected? That is why, Thegn Deormund, Sceapig needs a protector, someone to organise resistance. We cannot allow the isle to become a Norse base and a menace to the Kingdom of Kent beyond. I think that is clear enough, unless you wish to add anything, Thegn?"

The title did not sit right with him and he had plenty to say.

"Archdeacon, the islanders are no warriors. Men like my father are too old to face the Norsemen, others are too young and callow. They have farming implements, no match for the seasoned and disciplined raiders from overseas." He could have continued at length but halted when he saw the exchange of looks between the two men.

The archdeacon cleared his throat, took a deep breath and treated Deormund to a withering stare.

"Do not presume that we have not considered all of these aspects, young man, yet here we are, raising you to thegn. You are from good Jutish stock and will, I am sure, overcome these minor obstacles. Moreover, you can count on our support."

Deormund, who knew little of history, promised himself to ask his better-informed father.

Jutish stock? What does it mean?

The prelate cut across his thoughts. "We believe that you are the man to hold the island, your home, against Viking incursions. Nobody will force you to sign this document. You may renounce this opportunity, but I implore you to consider the consequences. Think of the women and children. You have a family to protect, I remember?"

"Enough!" Deormund's voice rang out, harsh and determined. "Where do I sign?"

The clergyman's cold demeanour melted like hailstones in the sun, to be replaced by a jubilant grin directed at Sibert. "We have our man, Sibert! Congratulations, you were right about our former deer herder."

Former deer herder?

He passed a quill to Deormund and slid an earthenware inkpot across the table. With spread-eagled fingers, he spun a document, sliding it across to the incredulous one-time ceorl. He skimmed the parchment, passing over his name coupled with the title *thegn*, noted the familiar place names, now his property, to settle finally upon the large, red wax seal attached by a crimson ribbon to the bottom of the document. Dipping the quill into the ink, he carefully drew the nib across the brim of the pot to remove excess black liquid before he scratched his signature across the page. The archdeacon removed the quill from his motionless grasp and handed it to Sibert, who signed his name with a flourish. The quill regained, Wulfred wrote his name followed by a stylised cross, then startled Deormund by bellowing, "You may enter now!"

Three awaiting priests came into the small room. In succession, they underwrote their names as witnesses and congratulated Thegn Deormund.

Ritual thanks over, the *simple ceorl* felt that he could easily adapt to his new responsibilities and, determined to demonstrate his worth, turned to Sibert as they left the cathedral. "Thegn Sibert, I will need to create a forge on Sceapig, but as you know, we have no smith capable of shaping weapons on the isle."

"Then you must seek one." Sibert smiled.

"But *you* have three in Faversham and one in Oare."

The thegn, no longer in a place of worship, raised his bearded chin and guffawed, causing a stray dog to snarl and bark.

"By all the saints, Deormund, you are worse than the Vikings. You will despoil me of all I own! I dare say you'll be begging to keep Wardric, before long."

"Now that you mention it—"

"I know! I'd already thought you'd need him to transform your islanders into warriors. You have my blessing, keep him— I'll be glad to be rid of the old grumbler," he lied, "and take the Oare smith, too. I can't part with Cynebald, but you'll be needing a good wheelwright, I presume."

Deormund grinned and nodded; it would be good to work with at least one of his brothers. He beamed at his former lord, uneasy about how to behave, then thrust out a hesitant hand, which the thegn clasped warmly.

"Don't worry. A stronger Sceapig is in the best interests of Faversham. All I ask is that you respond if I ever need your help. I know you are the right man, *Thegn Deormund*."

SIXTEEN

SCEAPIG

802 AD

DEORMUND BORROWED LONG TABLES FROM THE ABBEY refectory to have them laid out in the middle of the campsite outside the nunnery gates. In this way, he transformed the spartan place of linen tents, sweat and toil into a place of laughter and entertainment. Torches were lashed to poles and gave sputtering light as the day dimmed while the first stars glimmered in the black sky. Asculf, his special guest, worked the spit, sending dripping fat hissing into the fire, roasting the venison meal Deormund had promised. His father had slaughtered a deer and prepared and delivered it for the skewer.

Cyneflaed, having left little Asculf at home with Bebbe, organised a bevy of island women paid by her husband to act as servants for the evening. It suited his plan that their husbands came to the feast, too.

Deormund clapped his hands. "Bring the food. Tonight, I want dancing, music and laughter such as Sceapig has never known." At his words, a musician strummed his hearpe, his fine, mellow voice stilling the chattering tongues as he sang an ancient ballad about a faery princess and her magic arts. The meal began with a barley-broth soup before they served three steaming poached sea salmon. Thanks to a fortuitous catch by one of the islanders, the fish, placed one to each table, were a last-minute addition, simmered in white wine.

Deormund, at the centre of the bench nearest to the abbey, kept a watchful eye on his guests, impatient to spring his surprise. Carefully judging the moment to make his announcement, he allowed them to devour the venison with relish before battering the hilt of his seax on the table and standing. They had consumed sufficient ale and mead to be relaxed, but were not too far in their cups to be quarrelsome or uncomprehending.

"Friends, I have a declaration to make, which will come as a surprise even to my own family." He was aware of, but avoided, Cyneflaed's inquisitive gaze. Pressing on, he withdrew the charter from within his tunic, unrolled it to reveal the crimson seal and announced, "By the will of the landowner of Sceapig— that is, the Church, in the name of the Archbishop of Canterbury—I declare my nomination as Thegn of Sceapig."

He waited for the news to sink into the heads of the islanders present, gazing around to gauge their reactions. He saw mostly surprise and confusion, not the jubilation he had secretly wished for. Wardric, next to him, stood, raised his beaker and cried, "Long live the Thegn of Sceapig."

Too slowly, the assembly rose, lifted their cups and echoed the refrain.

"Louder! Let's hear some enthusiasm," the Dorset voice boomed: "Long live the Thegn of Sceapig." He repeated it three times, each time louder than the one before, until the cry resounded from the abbey walls, where the shouting had brought curious females to peer over the ramparts.

At last, there was conviction in the chanting and when Cyneflaed bent to kiss her now seated husband, a great cheer rent the air, followed by ribald comments unsuited to the proximity of the abbey. Cyneflaed blushed to the roots of her hair but beamed at the cheering menfolk.

Deormund stood again to speak, his voice authoritative. "Friends, I have grown up among you. Many will be asking the question, why should Asculf's son, a deer herder, no better than us, become our thegn? I will answer that at once. Because the deer herder slew the first Viking chieftain who dared to set foot on Sceapig to plunder our herds..." he paused to judge the mood and finding it curious, not querulous, he continued, "and because *I* led the men of Faversham through the Norse shield-wall at Lyminge. Also..." he waved a hand behind him airily, "I directed the work on those towers. Thegn Sibert, my friend, believes I am the man to defend Sceapig, and I—" he drew his sword with a flourish— "swear on this cross," he kissed the guard at the hilt, "that I will protect every man, woman and child on this isle."

A loud cheer, sincere this time, rang around the table. Standing in front of grinning faces, he knew he had convinced them of his worth. Now came the hard part, convincing them of *their* value. Waiting for the clamour to die down, he raised a hand to capture their attention again.

"Here next to me sits Wardric, a veteran of many campaigns. He is not a man of Kent but comes from Dorset. I learnt from him how to wield this blade and much more besides. Men of Sceapig, you, too, will learn to use axes and swords, forged in our new smithy on this island. Every able-bodied man will train to defend his home from the sea wolves." Only a couple of half-hearted cheers, tailing off in embarrassment, greeted this proclamation.

Asculf spoke for the older men.

"Son, many of us are too old and arthritic to be warriors. Do you expect me to face a battle-hardened warrior, expert in the use of weapons?"

"Asculf," he used his father's name for effect, "I expect you to defend your wife and home, aye, I do! You will learn that even a giant foe can be felled by cunning. The alternative is to be defenceless like one of your sheep, to allow everything you care for to be plundered and ravaged. Why do you think we built these towers? To pass the time?"

"I say you cannot form an army with old men and youths," Asculf insisted.

"That is what the Norsemen think. My task is to prove them wrong. Father, would you rather face a Viking with a shield and battle-axe to defend what's yours, or use the nearest sickle? Ay, for sure, that would end badly!" His raucous, disrespectful laugh was like a slap in the face. Asculf sat down, his face drawn and ashamed.

"But come, more ale!" Deormund called. "Bring sweets!" Stewed apples and pears sprinkled with crushed nuts and drizzled with honey arrived to cheer the shaken islanders.

"You'll have to ask Thegn Sibert for permission to let me train your rabble," Wardric murmured, close to Deormund's ear.

"I will not! You are my man now, Wardric." He placed a hand on the veteran's arm and fixed him with a penetrating stare. "It is agreed, I am your lord now, Wardric. Sibert has also given me the smith and wheelwright of Oare."

"Do I have no say in the matter?" growled Wardric.

"My old friend, my need is greater than Sibert's."

Wardric beamed and patted the hand on his forearm, "Then you shall have my help, but don't expect miracles with these old men and youths."

"You made me into a warrior, so you can do this. Don't underestimate the Sceapigas; these men are rugged and hard-working whilst island life is tough. They are often out in all weathers; many are used to lifting heavy weights. By the time you've finished with them, they'll give the Norsemen *gristle for their rotten teeth to chew!*"

Wardric laughed and said, "Very well, Thegn Deormund, but I'll expect more feasts like this one. You know that a thegn must have a hall, do you not?"

Deormund had not thought about that but Wardric was right. People would not look respectfully at a thegn who still lived with his parents. He fell silent to ponder where to build his hall. Suddenly, creating a new nucleus composed of the hall with a smithy, wheelwright and respective homes appealed to him. However, it would need a defensible position.

"What about here? Near the abbey?"

The elderly warrior furrowed his brow to consider the possibility.

"It's likely the best place on the isle. See yonder knoll? You could make that secure as it boasts the advantage of overlooking any approach to the nunnery from the beach below."

"By God's hooks, Wardric, you are right! When do you reckon we'll have finished at the abbey?"

"Another two days to strengthen the gates with a second layer of timber should be enough."

"Sibert need never know that his men are building my hall."

"Even if he finds out, you can tell him that it's not a hall but an outlying fortress to reinforce the abbey defences."

"There's some truth in that, old fox."

They crashed their beakers together and drank in a comradely contentment, Deormund sure of his man.

Work on the hall proceeded apace. By now, the Faversham labourers, used to felling, trimming and hauling from the nearby woodland, worked swiftly, creating a building sixty-five feet long and thirty-six wide. Deormund was satisfied that it would comfortably accommodate sixty people. The builders made use of poles obtained from earlier coppicing and a nogging technique between the timber uprights. At the end of three months, roof thatching began. Sceapig boasted an abundance of reeds in its marshes for the purpose.

The construction completed, Deormund organised a second feast, inviting all the islanders. Again, roasted meat was the main course, not venison but mutton and goat. The folks did not come empty-handed but brought gifts of sheepskins, woollen blankets and, the biggest surprise of all, his own coat of arms. Eored, his brother and wheelwright, had carved a wooden shield to be nailed over the door. He had painted the crest so that it showed boldly in the torchlight. It portrayed two stags rampant supporting a central shield, its motif depicted in blue and white zigzags to represent the water of the Swale. Eored had displayed his work to others before Deormund saw it. Two of the island women entered the hall, carrying a pole. One of them held a white cloth around the end of the spar. When she reached the thegn, she called to her husband to push the wood upright. As he did so, she shook the pole so that the linen fell free to reveal an attached embroidered banner—the same emblem as Eored's painted wooden boss. A great cheer rose to the rafters, followed by the rhythmic chanting of *"Long live Deormund, Thegn of Sceapig!"*

In his only speech of the evening, Deormund called for one last building effort. He ordered a palisade to be built around the hall with one simple lookout tower on the seaward prospect of the knoll.

"The enclosure will be large enough to contain a smithy, several workshops," he stared pointedly at Eored, who beamed his approval, "stables, sties and, I hope, one day, a well."

The last construction rose towards the end of the autumn

in the shape of the new forge. The Oare blacksmith, a stubborn, red-haired fellow named Sherred, had required much persuasion by Thegn Sibert to transfer to Sceapig. The warm welcome provided him by the islanders, who would no longer have to travel to find a smith, and the consignment of a boatload of iron bars, removed the last traces of the sullenness he displayed on arrival.

"Sherred, Thegn Sibert tells me that you crafted his sword?" Deormund made it sound like a question, but it was a statement.

"Ay, Lord, that I did. Will you be wanting me to make one for you?" the smith asked doubtfully, eying the weapon hanging at his thegn's side.

"One? Nay, I'll want forty."

"Forty?"

"I see all your hammering has not deafened you, my friend. *Forty*. Temper the blades well. We will need them in battle in the years to come. No need for fancy work, just serviceable against one of these. He whipped out his Viking sword and pressed it lightly against the smith's leather jerkin."

Sherred's eyes narrowed as he lifted the blade away with outstretched fingers, all the while appraising the steel.

"It'll have to be my best work, Lord, to compare with steel such as yours."

"You will be well rewarded, Sherred the Smith. You don't know it yet, but you are one of the most important men on this isle in my eyes. Forty swords are just the beginning. See that you fit in the day-to-day items the islanders ask of you, too."

The smith nodded, a serious expression on his swarthy face. He liked the plain-talking thegn. This lord might be young, but he knew how to make a man feel valued. He would have his forty swords sooner than he thought.

Deormund was walking out of the forge, but a call from the smith brought him back,

"Lord, I'll be needing another load of iron bars." He nodded toward the neat stack in the back of the smithy.

"Ay, you will. Good job I ordered them when these arrived." He turned away with a smile. From the smith's face, he knew he had gained a friend.

———

THE HARVEST GATHERED IN, the deer safely penned, Deormund saw out the autumn by supervising Wardric's weapons training. One day, the veteran called to him.

"Don't just stand there, Thegn, come, test your mettle against my champion!"

The Dorset man had been preparing the islanders for months. Deormund knew what that meant and did not envy the trainees. He strolled over to the beaten earth training area.

"Unbuckle your weapon and give it to me. Grab a shield and practice sword. Ready?" The question was directed at an islander whose face was hidden behind his shield.

"Ay!" came the gruff reply.

Deormund closed on his opponent, wooden sword raised and, since he could not study his adversary's eyes, kept a steady gaze at his feet, noting every movement. Suddenly, his foe sprang forward, catching him by surprise but Deormund smashed his shield into the aggressor's so that he staggered away. They hacked and parried for long minutes, the other man still holding his shield in an unusually high position. The thegn tired of the game, deciding to make the fellow pay for his presumption. Casting his shield aside to distract his challenger, Deormund threw himself to the ground, rolled and slashed at the exposed legs before him.

"Ow! Damn you! I'll not walk for a month!" The thunderous face of Asculf emerged from behind the linden barrier.

"Father! You fight well, but let that be a lesson to hold your shield lower."

"You used cunning!" the shepherd grumbled.

"Ay," laughed Wardric, gazing around the interested faces, "and that's another lesson learnt. Expect the unexpected! Your enemies do not pretend to have fine manners: they will want to slice into your flesh, to spill the brains from your skulls or the guts from your bellies! They will use any ploy they can."

Deormund strode to his father. "Are you all right?"

"Next time, it'll be *you* hobbling home to your hall!"

Deormund grinned and said, "At last, we are ready for the Norsemen. Let them come!"

SEVENTEEN
SCEAPIG
803 AD

OFTEN WORDS ARE CHEAP, THROWAWAY REMARKS OR, AS
with Deormund's reassurance that they were ready for the
Vikings, calculated only to raise morale. After the Yuletide
festivities, the persistence of the winter gloom transformed the
estuary landscape into an unbroken heron grey continuum of
water and sky. The damp penetrated the islanders' bones;
everything dripped water and people yearned for the onset of
spring—except for Deormund. The arrival of spring, he knew,
would lift the woe but would replace that emotion with worry.
If the Norsemen arrived on Sceapig, would his youths and
greybeards have any chance of stopping them? In his heart and,
worse, his head, he knew that there was little hope.

Thankfully, he did not have time to spend every waking
hour brooding and fretting. The elrick was packed with deer.
His father had spent the last two years pampering the beasts
and, however grudgingly he had to admit it, Asculf had a way
with animals. At the last count, the enclosure contained sixty
beasts. Were so many sustainable on this isle? He doubted it
and, with heavy heart, considered the prospect of a cull later in

the year. In a separate pen, his stag thrived in the company of the subdued hart. The satisfaction of seeing the old rivals rub along in harmony cheered him. Two male calves, wisely separated from the hinds by Asculf now they were two years old, completed that compound. The young males strutted around imitating the dominant male, who tolerated them with great patience, aware of his supremacy in the herd. Careful animal husbandry had paid dividends, for, despite the cramped conditions of the deer, the animals were lively and in robust health. That, thought Deormund, was one worry less.

Since he could not sit outdoors on his favourite boulder where he did his best thinking, and was no longer living in his parents' home, he sat on the low, circular wall surrounding the hearth in his hall, where he absorbed the warmth of the log fire. Idly stroking Mistig's shaggy ear, he indulged his anxieties, fretting about an imagined Norse raid.

His mind went back to his first encounter with the Vikings. On that occasion, they had left the ashes of their chieftain on Sceapig. Marvelling that they had not yet returned to sate a desire for vengeance, he considered it only a matter of time. He shifted his hand to run a thumb gently between the hound's eyes, causing Mistig to raise a huge paw and place it on his knee. Why could a man not be left alone to live in peace with his animals? Deormund did not pause to think that the Vikings were doing what his forebears had done: raiding another country for the riches their starved land could not provide. He put his thoughts into words for the benefit of his canine companion.

"Oh, aye, they'll return all right, Mistig." The dog's tail thumped the floor. "They know there are easy pickings on Sceapig where the landing is safe. The problem is, how will we fight them off?"

The dark eyes of the hound bored into his as if trying to

provide the answer. He repeated the question silently in his head, but this time stressed the 'we'—how will *we* fight them off? That was the revelational moment when the idea came to him. Mistig would not need much special training, either. It would be easy for the dog to adapt.

Feeling much less anxious, Deormund stood, his demeanour determined. Mistig, sensing his mood, bounded to the door and soon they were hastening together to his father's home. Once there, he cut a seasoned sausage into treat-sized chunks for the hound before putting them in his pocket. Outside, he unlatched the gate of the stags' compound, released the dominant male, but kept the other three inside the pen.

"Go on, Mistig, chase him to the meadow, fast!"

The dog tilted his grey head and gazed inquiringly at his master, who waved both arms impatiently, flicking his hands outwards. "Go on! After him! Quickly!"

The deer was already grazing, but Mistig startled the skittish beast with a bark and then pursued the stag, growling hard on its heels. "Faster, Mistig, faster!" Deormund cried, running after them. "Good boy! Stop!" He pulled out his whistle and blew a blast, causing the hound to skid to a halt on the wet grass, sending a spray of surface water arcing upwards. The stag, aware that his tormentor had stopped his pursuit, slowed to a standstill and stood gazing warily at the dog and its master.

Deormund rewarded his companion with a treat and a hug. "That's it, Mistig, that's what I want! Now go, chase him home. Go on!"

At first his head cocked to one side, considering, but then, in a grey flash, the deerhound was away, barking and snapping at the stag's heels. Again, the dog drove the deer at breakneck speed across the wet ground, twisting and turning the nimble beast by snarling at its flanks until it flew in the direction the hound wanted—homewards. Another reward came the faithful hound's way after Deormund had closed the door of the pen on the panting deer.

The exercise had been a success, as well as much-needed, for both hound and stag. The deer herder was lavish in his praise. He squatted to hug his shaggy grey friend, smothering him with caresses and feeding him his favourite treat. "We'll do the same tomorrow, boy," he paused, "and the day after."

These practices went well, but Deormund decided not to develop his idea further for the moment. He figured that it would work better as a complete surprise for everybody, always assuming that it would be needed.

———

SPRING WAS CHANGING the aspect of the isle as fresh green shoots abounded. The deer and sheep were back on the meadow. Deormund took great pleasure in observing the behaviour of his herd. Asculf likely derived greater satisfaction from the lambing. Soon, many young animals were frisking and dancing across the lea.

Deormund divided his time between herding and thegn duties. Held in deep respect by the islanders, the latter became a more demanding commitment. The island community was close-knit so that friendship, ties of kin and animosities were deeply felt. The hostilities, traditionally resolved with no outside participation, occasionally led to long-standing feuds. Since the acceptance of Deormund as thegn, the people brought minor disputes to him. His impartiality and wisdom were common knowledge, as he had settled arguments over the retrieval of flotsam, mooring rights and even one paternity case.

On this occasion, two men he had known since infancy were almost at blows over the right to collect shellfish in a cove.

"My house is nearer than Wilgar's, so I reckon the cockles

and whelks on that stretch of shore are mine by rights, Thegn," said Osred.

"Whatever the sea gifts us can be claimed by any man, Lord. It is of no matter where his house stands," argued Wilgar.

Deormund rose from his carved seat, made by his brother Eored and turned to cross the hall to a locked cupboard. From there, he withdrew a document of deeds retrieved from the abbey. Knowing that neither man could read, he spread it on the table to make a great show of reading aloud.

"Ah, here it is, the cove in question," he lied. "Well, well, that sheds a different light on matters."

They had drawn near to peer over his shoulder, but the writing meant nothing except black shapes to them.

"The law must have the last word, my friends, and it states here that the inlet and its beach belong to the landowner. In this case, to me. That makes my decision much easier, Osred. I am as partial to seafood as any man; therefore, this is my judgment. Since your house is nearest to the cove," Wilgar's eyes narrowed, "you may collect whatever shellfish you find this week. On the last day of the month, you will collect them and bring them to my kitchen."

He turned to Wilgar. "My friend, you will do the same and supply my table." With a smile first, he added, "Next month it will be your turn, so you know what to do on the last day of the month. Thenceforth, you will alternate. If either of you fails to fetch my share at the appointed time, you will lose the right granted this day."

"What if the last day of a month is a storm, Lord?"

Deormund chortled and gazed at Osred, "Good question. In that case, I'll ascribe it to God not wanting me to eat His whelks!"

All three laughed, with the two men leaving the hall old friends as before the dispute. Deormund watched them leave with a smile, content that he would receive shellfish without bending his back. *May the Lord forgive my little lies.*

He had become expert at turning disputes to his advantage. The most serious case involved his father's sheep. Asculf came to him with the grave accusation that three brothers from the south-east side of the island, Harty, had stolen six of his lambs at night. Deormund buckled his sword and accompanied his father to the brothers' pasture.

The three strong young men, each wielding a staff, swaggered up to father and son.

"What do you want?" one snarled.

Deormund drew his sword, noting how the brothers readied their staves.

"First of all, I am your thegn and you will address me with a civil tongue. Second, you'll lay down those staves or risk your lives. Need I remind you that I have a score of armed men at my beck and call?"

The one who had addressed him rudely made a show of looking around. "I see only one old man," he sneered.

"I'm losing my patience," Deormund snapped. Mistig settled onto his haunches and growled menacingly, his face contorting to reveal a curved fang.

With a cry and a rush, the lout attacked, but he'd reckoned without Asculf, who tossed his walking stick between the onrushing man's legs, bringing him crashing to the ground. In a flash, Deormund was standing over him with his blade pressed to the scoundrel's throat.

"Stand back and throw down your staves, or he dies!"

Asculf bent to pick up one of the sturdy staves, readying it if need be, whilst Mistig, growling threateningly, eyed the pair.

"You three are accused of stealing six lambs by night from my father."

"You have no proof of that, Lord," the eldest of the brothers said, but his tone was unconvincing and worried.

"Father, take Mistig and round up your animals. You two, do not move an inch, else my blade will slit his throat."

Whilst his father was away on the pasture, Deormund, using his deepest, most authoritative voice, declared, "This is what will happen. We will show the lambs are my father's, then, you will accompany me, without weapons, to my hall to stand trial before twelve good men."

"A lamb's a lamb. You can't prove a thing, Thegn."

"We'll soon see."

To the sound of bleating, Asculf arrived followed by six frisky lambs carefully marshalled by the watchful and energetic deerhound.

"Show the thieves, Father!"

Asculf scooped up one of the lambs and carried it to the eldest rogue,

"Look," he said, gently flattening out an ear. "I nocked the ears, just to be sure no thieves would escape with my lambs. Do you still say these are your animals?"

Resigned, the brothers exchanged glances and shook their heads, hanging them simultaneously. They were caught, for they hadn't noticed. Their lambs had no ear-nocking to prove their innocence.

"On your feet." Deormund removed the blade but did not sheath his sword. "You three are coming to the hall, where I'll decide what to do with you. Father, you are an expert with a staff; keep an eye on them. Next time, my steel will not stay dry, so it's best you believe me. Drive them home, Mistig!"

The men travelled in silence, the brothers worrying about the thegn's judgment, sure to be severe. Safely back home, Asculf ordered the hound to drive the lambs to the flock on the meadow. When they arrived at the hall, Deormund surprised them by asking to see their hands. Anxiously, the men held them out before him. With a deliberately savage smile, the deer herder told them to turn them so he could inspect both sides. The three men cowered, knowing that a common punishment for theft was to lose a hand.

Six islanders sat either side of Deormund at his high table. The three miscreants, heads bowed, stood below and in front. Arrayed behind them, Wardric, with five armed guards, completed the assembly.

Deormund asked his father to relate in detail what had happened earlier. At the end, the shepherd explained the ear-nocking proof, which was conclusive. Deormund spoke in a ringing voice, "Men of the jury, raise your right hand if you find these three men guilty."

Twelve hands rose in unison.

"The jury has found you guilty of theft, which means I must pronounce judgement. The law is clear: a thief must lose his right hand so that he may not steal again. Also," he stared at the youngest and hardened his voice, "a man who wilfully attacks his lord, according to King Ine's law, forfeits his life."

The shocked silence that greeted his words made Deormund's mouth twitch at the corner.

"Take them into the yard!"

The brothers expected to lose a hand, the other his head and they made a pitiful sight, especially the youngest, who had wet his breeches.

"I inspected your hands earlier," Deormund said. "They are honest worker's hands: hard and calloused, perfect for what I have in mind. You have heard the sentence; as your thegn, the law allows me to execute it, but God in His mercy has given me a better idea."

Wardric raised an eyebrow; it would never do to show mercy to thieves.

"I will give you the choice: lose two hands and a head or accept this offer." Deormund strode deeper into the courtyard, drew his sword and to everyone's surprise, scratched a circle in the earth. "Here, you will dig every day from dawn to dusk, with a break only for a midday meal. Only when you reach fresh water will you stop. I want you to dig me a well." This was a project close to his heart since the hall was reliant on collected rainwater, or water carted in a barrel from the abbey well.

"Bless you, Lord!" The youngest was on his knees, tears of relief streaming down his face.

"Not so fast. All three must be in agreement and you must each swear never to steal throughout the rest of your lives."

"Lord," said the eldest, "I agree and vow never to steal again."

"I too, Lord, and thank you, Thegn."

The youngest stood slowly, "You have spared my life, Thegn Deormund. I will serve you faithfully and never rob henceforth."

"Good. Fetch picks, spades, and buckets! You will work until dusk. Wardric, watch over them. They have yet to win my trust. Tend to your sheep, Father. Take Mistig to help you."

"You have a wise head; I'm proud of you, my son. Come on, boy!"

With a thrill of pleasure as the first pick dug into the ground, another thought occurred to Deormund.

If ever I'm besieged by Vikings in this hall, I'll have water to drink or to quench flames.

He desperately hoped to find fresh water and use it only for drinking.

EIGHTEEN
SCEAPIG
802-803 AD

DEORMUND'S CONSTANT CHECKING WITH THE LOOKOUT tower was a source of amusement among his men, but apart from two false alarms, the months slid quietly by, untroubled by Viking presence. Gradually, the deer herder's anxiety lulled till his preoccupation became the well. From the first day of digging, when the brothers found it easy work as they formed a spoil heap of thick sand, soon followed by the same containing flint pebbles, he had overseen their progress. Doubts began to assail him when they struggled with the fresh, bluish-grey clay. Their tools lodged into the energy-sapping material, whose suction made them curse and sweat. Occasionally, their lord reminded them that this toil was a punishment, and as such, far better than losing a hand or a head.

One day, accompanying his brother's cart and water barrel to the abbey, he chanced upon the prioress. From their first meeting, he had liked her, finding her easy to talk to. He confided his worries about the well.

"Thegn Deormund, I would not fret on that score. Your

hall is much on the same land level as the abbey. Did you know that there is another well in our grounds? Come, I will show you. It is considered holy since it was blessed by Saint Seaxburh, our foundress."

Deormund received this news with joy. After all, if there were two wells, should there not be hope for a third? She took him to the confines of the courtyard and pointed to a covered, stone-ringed circle.

"You may remove the cover if you so desire, Thegn, but it is hardly worth the effort just to peer down a well."

"I disagree, Sister, since I'd like to gauge its depth by lowering the bucket. It might tell me how deep my diggers will need to go."

She smiled and said, "You can take off the wooden covering."

"Come, Eored, lend a hand!"

They laid the heavy oak platform aside to peer into the depths. Nearby stood a pail attached to a rope. Eored seized it and let it down carefully, paying out yards of hempen cord until he expressed himself satisfied that the bucket had sunk into the water.

"Haul it up, brother. Have a care to measure the cord."

The prioress peered into the well, watching the slow upward progress of the pail. Her voice reverberated in the well. "We use the waters from the magical well for drinking and bathing the wounds of injured people, and sometimes even animals, thus effecting outstanding cures among the sick and injured."

Deormund replied, "I do not seek such miracles. I want nothing but fresh water for my people."

"You will have it, Thegn, have faith—have you prayed for a successful outcome?"

"Every night, Sister."

"Then, I will add my prayers to yours at Vespers."

Eored grasped the bucket. "I make those roughly sixty-six feet."

"Twenty-two yards," Deormund muttered. "Interesting."

Prioress Leowen, less concerned about the thegn's well, was thinking about her own. "During my time here, Thegn, a desperate woman not blessed with a child came to us after a series of miscarriages. We bade her drink of this well and lo! She now has a fine son. Is that not a miracle?"

Deormund cupped his fingers in the water and drank, smacking his lips and drying his beard with the cuff of his sleeve.

"Indeed, it is, Prioress. I hope that our water will be as cool and clear as this, should we ever strike lucky."

"Have faith." She laid a hand on his arm, her so-familiar reassuring grey eyes imploring him.

"I'm sure you are right, Sister, and when we do, I will come here to let you know."

Later, in the hall courtyard, he shouted to the younger of the brothers, the one who would have walked over hot coals if called upon to do so for the lord who had spared his life.

He tossed a coiled rope at the bewildered young man. "Here, use this to measure down; I want to know how deep you've dug."

"At once, Thegn!"

A few words of explanation to his brother in the hole and the other hauling up the spoil bucket, then, he lowered the end of the rope while Deormund looked on with interest. Reversing the operation, re-coiling the cord, the erstwhile shepherd-turned-thief counted off the feet: forty-eight, forty-nine, *fifty!*

"We're down fifty feet, Lord."

Deormund walked to the hole and peered down to see a grimy, grinning face looking up at him.

"The clay's wetter down here," the man called up.

"I'm back from the abbey well. If ours is the same, you should hit the rock in about ten feet. That's when our well will fill. Can you swim?" he joked.

The elder brother laughed and yelled, "If I don't drown, I'll freeze to death down here."

"When you release the water, the three of you will be free to tend your sheep."

Since becoming a thegn, his worries had multiplied. As a way of life, worrying was pointless and unproductive. But what if the water was brackish, undrinkable? If only his faith was as strong as that of the prioress! Her prayers must have helped because, after a fortnight of combatting the ever-more resistant clay, now slimy and cloying, the brothers released the groundwater pressure. The second brother, whose turn it was to dig, yelped and hauled himself up the rope, his breeches and shoes dripping wet but with a beam of triumph on his face.

"We've done it! There's water in the well. Call Thegn Deormund!"

"I'll go," cried the youngest and hared off to the hall.

The guard at the door was the imposing Eadlac, who had pleaded with Sibert to let him remain with his friend, the new thegn.

"Hey, you! Where do you think you're going in that state? Can't have you trailing muck into the thegn's hall."

"I have tidings Thegn Deormund will wish to hear."

"Do you, indeed?" Both men turned to see the smiling thegn standing in the doorway. "The news I want to hear is that there's water in my well."

The young man could barely contain his excitement as he hopped from one foot to the other, "There is, Lord! We did it!"

"Wait there!" Deormund emerged a moment later clutching a beaker, "Let's taste the quality of our water."

Ordering a bucket to be lowered, he grasped the cup so tightly that his knuckles whitened. Would the water be drinkable? The pail appeared, slopping water as it bumped against the wall of the well.

"We'll have to build a winch," he muttered, grasping the handle of the pail to set it down at his feet. He stared at the water and smiled. At least it wasn't murky from the excavated clay; it appeared crystal clear. Presumably, the detritus would have sunk to the bottom of the well. He dipped his beaker into the liquid and felt the coolness of the water on his hand. The faces of the brothers and that of Eadlac, who had abandoned his post out of curiosity, peered at him eagerly. He drew a mouthful and swilled it around before mischievously spitting it out. Seeing the disappointed faces, he bellowed a laugh. "It's sweet!" Noticing the wet breeches for the first time, he handed the full beaker to the man who had hit water. "Here, try it! You must have a thirst."

Regarding the vessel with suspicious eyes, the shepherd did no more than take a sip, but then smiled and guzzled down the lot. "Our water's pure!" he announced.

"You have done fine work. Your punishment ends here. Consider this, though; honest toil brings righteous rewards, often not measured in coins or goods, but the invisible currency of esteem. Mark my words, from enmity you have gained my favour. Now, go, tend your sheep."

Amid thanks, smiles and forelock-tugging, Deormund thought about the well again.

"Hold! One more thing." He beckoned the man with damp breeches. "What rock did you reach?"

"It looked like chalk to me, Lord."

"All right, good, I'll keep you no longer from your home."

Moments later, Eored appeared in the doorway of his workshop, rolling out a newly iron-banded cartwheel.

"Oi, brother! Over here!" *Just the man I need.*

"What's the matter, Thegn?"

Deormund glared at him. "How many times must I tell you? You will call me by name."

Eored grinned mischievously. "Very well, Thegn Deormund!"

"One of these days, I swear I'll slit that tongue of yours!"

Eored chuckled; he enjoyed tormenting his brother. Despite his playacting, he truly admired Deormund's leadership qualities. "So, what's the matter?"

Deormund held out a beaker freshly filled from the pail. "Here, try this. We have water in our compound, brother."

Quick to realise the implications, Eored enthused about the benefits and quality of the water.

"The digger told me he thought he had reached the bedrock—possibly chalk."

"It *is* chalk."

"How can you be so sure?"

Remember when we were boys and played down there?" He indicated with a tilt of his head. "It was a hot day when you pointed up the cliff to a spring gushing from the rock. We climbed up to drink—"

The thegn grinned. "You're right, brother, the spring gushed forth just above the chalk seam. I wonder if it's still there? I don't recall seeing it in recent times."

"Springs come and go; it depends on the movements underground. I'll check for you if you like. It would be a shame to waste good water. A spring can be blocked or channelled."

"I have another job for you." He went on to suggest the building of a frame to support a winch.

151

"First, have some men build a wall around the hole, before some drunken wretch stumbles into it on a moonless night."

Eored agreed. "I'll speak with Sherred; he can make the winch handle in metal and, at the same time, I'll stock up on nails." He set off to do that.

Wardric wandered over, his Dorset burr forming into a complaint. "Well, young master, you've worked another miracle, I see. But why only water? I thought you might provide an ale well at the very least." His blue eyes twinkled.

"Old rogue! I know when you're after my best ale. Come along, then, never let it be said that I mistreat my oldest friends. Eadlac! Fetch Eored; we need trusty drinking companions!" The guard beamed at his thegn. Sibert had been a fine lord, but this one was also a friend. It didn't bear thinking that he had once been charged with harming him.

The creation of a new well was cause for celebration. Excusing himself for dampening the cheerful mood, Wardric turned to Eored. "When you've finished constructing the winch, why don't you build a rack with ten fire buckets? God knows, I hope we never need them, but it's as well to be prepared. If we're ever under siege, the besiegers are sure to fire blazing arrows to force us out." He looked anxiously at Deormund, not wishing to usurp his authority. He need not have worried.

"Eored, from a mere wheelwright, you are becoming an indispensable woodworker. I'll see you are well rewarded for your efforts."

"Don't worry, brother, Cyneflaed sees to it that my family lacks for nothing; she and Saewynn are forever with their heads pressed together. Goodness knows how much your wife has raided from your larder. She's worse than a Viking!"

Deormund chuckled but, despite the ale, anxiety was clawing at his gut. First, talk of fire buckets, and now, mention of Vikings. The Norsemen had been too quiet for his peace of mind. Maybe he'd cross the Swale to see what news Sibert had. The thegn was in constant contact with Archdeacon Wulfred, a man whose finger was on the pulse of events, even those happening overseas. Anyway, he hadn't seen Cynebald and Wilgiva for some time. His nieces would soon be young women if he let more time slip away.

"I'm going over to Faversham for a few days. Eadlac, you can accompany me. You'll want to meet up with some of our old comrades; besides, I might need your muscles. When we return, I want to see the well completed, Eored, and my larder not depleted. I won't expect you to make all the buckets in three days; concentrate on the well winch."

"Ay, Theg—er—Deormund."

"Oh, one other thing. The day after tomorrow, go over to our parents. They were complaining that they hadn't seen their granddaughter for a while."

"They know I'm busy, why don't they come up to the hall?"

"A son must please his parents, Eored. Why do you think I'm going to Faversham? I'm going to stir Cynebald and Wilgiva to do their duty, too." He lied again. What had happened to the once honest, bluff deer herder? Lately, he found that he was always telling little lies to convince people to do what he considered best. *Am I right to be like this? Is this what responsibility brings?*

Thegn Deormund left the others to their ale and wandered into the courtyard. He looked up at the tall lookout tower and called, "All clear?" to his watchman.

"Ay, Lord!" Of course, it was; otherwise, he'd have heard the shrill alarm blast from the horn chained to a stanchion. One day, that alarm signal would come, he was sure of it. In truth, anything was better than this uncertainty gnawing away at his nerves. He would almost welcome pitting himself against the crew of a longship, whatever the cost.

Nay, not so. Some prices were too high to pay. He thought of his wife and son. Surely, their safety was at the root of this festering foreboding. At his hip, Mistig whined and gazed up. The deerhound was sensitive to his master's mood. Deormund sighed as he fondled the hound's ears, wishing he could live in the present like his dog and not have to worry about the future.

NINETEEN
SCEAPIG
803 AD

Whilst his thegn brother was away at Faversham, Eored finished the well canopy, complete with a winch. Nearby, he had also erected a standing frame fitted with ten hooks ready to receive the buckets he still had to make. Surveying his handiwork, he grunted with satisfaction before taking a well-earned break.

His childhood memory of the spring gushing from the cliff face lingered, so he chose to wander down to the beach to check whether there was still some outflow. Whistling cheerfully, he might have passed the mound of seaweed on the high-tide mark had it not been for Mistig's bouncing and yapping insistence. What had disturbed the deerhound to make him so jittery? Eored strode over to inspect the brown-green kelp and stopped in his tracks because a foot was poking out from under the fronds. Not a dead seal, then. The wheelwright eyed the drag mark that ran from the sea up to the edge of the shingle. Someone had hauled himself out of the waves and now lay before him unmoving on the beach.

Aided by the exuberant hound, Eored began to uncoil and pull away the strands of kelp. At last, they revealed the tall figure of a blond-haired man. Was he alive or dead? He must have been conscious when he dragged himself thus far. The islander bent down and shook the man's shoulder, but there was no response. Placing the tips of two fingers on the castaway's neck, he detected a faint pulse, so he was barely breathing!

Unbuckling a clasp on his cloak, Eored took it off and wrapped it over the damp, cold body, issuing the instruction, "Stay with him, Mistig!"

The hound lay down next to the man by his side, as if knowing that his body heat would warm the fellow. Eored raced away along the beach, taking the quickest route up to the hall. There, he grabbed a beaker and a leather bottle of cider, ordered a servant to light a fire, then called for Eadlac.

Quickly explaining the situation to the muscular bodyguard before they ran to the shore, they found everything unchanged except that Mistig leapt up to greet them with wagging tail.

"Sit him up, Eadlac."

As the man's upper body became upright, he spluttered and seawater poured out of his mouth, followed by coughs. His eyes opened and he coughed up more water.

"Get him up!"

Eadlac set the bottle and beaker on the shingle and helped the guard haul the man to his feet. Immediately, the castaway bent double and retched, the last of the salt water spouting from his mouth and splashing at their feet. "Hold him steady!"

The wheelwright retrieved the bottle of cider, unstopped it and held it to the man's lips. The brew filled his mouth, dribbled at the corners, but the fellow swallowed it eagerly. His eyes regained a spark of life; hitherto dull and emotionless, now they scanned the faces of the rescuers while colour returned slowly to his pallid cheeks. He took the bottle from Eored's hand and drew a long draught that set him off coughing and spluttering again, but he recovered his speech.

"Thank you, friends," he said in their tongue, but with a strong Norse accent. Despite the rescue, Eadlac's hand drifted to his sword hilt. Unseen by the Viking, Eored silently intimated *nay* with his eyes to the guard.

"Come, we'll take you to some warmth," the wheelwright said, retrieving the fallen cloak and wrapping it around the man before ducking under his arm and indicating that Eadlac should do the same. Together, they half-lifted, half-dragged him along the beach, then up to the hall.

Mistig followed meekly behind, having collected the beaker in his mouth. This self-appointed task sobered his exuberance, as normally, he would have charged ahead. They sat their guest in front of the crackling log fire, where the hound dropped the beaker and looked expectantly at Eored for a treat.

"Later, Mistig, let's hear our visitor's tale, it'll be worth the hearing." Instead, he ordered a servant to fetch a hot broth from the kitchen and a piece of sausage for the dog, who understood the word 'sausage' and beat his tail against their guest's calf.

The two Saxons sat on the hearth wall, either side of the shivering Norseman, careful not to mask the heat of the fire.

"How came you to be on our beach, *Viking?*"

The man looked anxiously from one face to the other for signs of the hostility the word bore.

"You ought to know," he said haltingly, "that I am not a warrior."

Eadlac smiled. "That accounts for the soft arms I felt around my shoulders This one's never wielded a battle-axe in his life."

"It's true, I swear by Odin, or by your God." He gazed anxiously at them.

"So, what kind of man are you?"

"A skald."

Eadlac gave Eored a puzzled look.

"That would be our scop. A musician, are you?"

"Ay, and as a bard, I know all our sagas. I'd be happy to play for you, by way of thanks for saving me."

The wheelwright smiled. "Our lord will be pleased to hear you when he returns this evening."

"I thought you were the lord of this hall. You command the servants."

"I am the lord's brother. Here's your broth; it should revive your spirits, Scop."

"Skald. Thank you."

Eadlac, who was studying the castaway with a curious expression, asked Eored, "What do you think a Norse scop was doing half-drowned in the sea?"

"Your guess is as good as mine. We'll let him drink his broth, then he can tell his tale."

"By Thor! That was the best broth of my life."

Eored bellowed a laugh. "Only because you needed it so badly, sco... skald. It was venison broth made from island deer."

"Is this an isle, then?"

"Ay, you are on Sceapig in the Kingdom of Kent."

"I've heard tell of Kent. So, this is not Frankia?"

The two men on the hearth wall roared with laughter. Eored wiped a tear of mirth from his eye with his sleeve and asked, "Why would you think that?"

"Well, it was to Frankia we were bound. A storm blew up out of nothing and we had to lower our sail and man the oars to prevent the ship from smashing on the rocks. We lost our mast in the blast so that when it blew itself out, we were helpless except for the oars. The sea calmed and our men rowed away from the Frankish coast. The next morning, not long after sunrise, our lookout spied two vessels sailing towards us. Ordinarily, we would easily have out-sailed them but, you see, we had no sail."

The scop looked miserably from one to the other, seeking sympathy where none was to be found. Neither pitied the Vikings. Undeterred, the scop continued, "They soon caught us, especially because our warriors had stopped rowing to prepare their weapons. Grappling hooks hauled us tightly against their ships. The Franks, all in chain armour, poured aboard and the most awful slaughter took place." The scop shuddered and his expression changed to one of horror as he recalled the events.

"But surely you, a Viking, are used to combat and the butchery of men?"

The musician shook his head. "As I said, I am no warrior and this was my first time overseas. My chieftain ordered me to leave our village and sail with him. I'm no sailor, either, if it comes to that!"

"Did the Franks win the day?"

The skald's eyes widened. "Ay, they spared no-one. I was hiding in the bows. When I saw them break through to advance on me, I flung myself overboard. I learnt to swim in the fjord as a child, so I thought my chances were greater in the cold water than under a sword blade."

"You cannot have swum here from Frankia!"

"True. I clung on to a branch I came across after a while and drifted towards Angle-land. Even so, I would not have made it this far but for the appearance of a small boat. The Saxons aboard hauled me out of the water."

"If those Saxons saved you, why were you on our beach?" Eored asked, suspicion in his voice.

"I heard them talking. One of them said that his lord hated Vikings. They joked about what he might do to me. So, I pretended I didn't understand their language." He shuddered again. "As soon as I saw the coast, I dived overboard and swam away, but my strength failed, so I had to float on my back. I reckon I passed out with the cold, but thanks to the All-Seeing One, here I am. Does your lord hate Vikings, too?"

"There's no love lost," Eadlac growled.

"But he is a generous man." Eored glared at his friend. "I dare say he could use a good scop."

"*Skald.* And I *am* good."

"As to that, we'll see later, at dinner tonight. Here, drink the rest of this cider. Brewed from local apples. Tell me, what is your name?"

"I am Torfi," but he seemed more intent on the cider than conversation.

Mistig stared at Eored's closed fist and drooled.

"You're right, old fellow; I've been holding on to this sausage all this time. I've neglected you."

The hound devoured the meat and looked hungrily at his master's brother. "There's no more, look!" He held out his hand to have it assiduously licked until there was no trace of the delicious grease. Then, before Eored's startled eyes, even as the dog finished the scrupulous operation, he flew like a slingshot across the hall to the door—a sure sign that his master had arrived.

Ritual fussing of the frenzied hound over, Deormund walked over to the hearth. "I see we have a visitor. Welcome, stranger."

The Norseman stood and bowed. "Well met, Lord."

His accent betrayed him, causing Deormund's eyes to narrow. "A Norseman?"

The Viking replied for himself, his voice now louder and more confident as he regained his strength. "Ay, Lord, a skald from the fjords of the far north. Your brother and his friend saved me from a certain death in the clutches of the sea."

"A skald?" Deormund wondered.

"A scop, brother."

"Ah, a musician—well, doubly welcome! You will sing for us. But tell me, how is it that you speak our language so well?"

The skald's expression became shifty and uncertain. He thought for a moment to find the right words.

"You see, in our village, we had a Saxon serving maid whom I befriended. Since she could not speak our tongue, I learnt hers. She also taught me one of your ballads. I'll sing it for you this evening if you have a hearpe."

"A serving maid?" Deormund's tone was cutting and dangerous. "A *slave*, more like, snatched from her home and family by Viking raiders."

This thegn was no fool. The skald had realised that he might reach this conclusion, which was the reason for his discomfiture.

"As I explained," he waved a hand at the other two, "I am no warrior. Neither am I a raider. They forced me to board the ship against my will."

Deormund, a good judge of character, was inclined to believe the bard.

"Let us make a pact, scop. You may stay here under my protection for as long as you like, but you will be in my employ and entertain us every evening unless we like not your cater-wauling."

The bard laughed but, just as suddenly, his face grew serious.

"I thank you for your hospitality, Thegn; I have no worries about my talent except..." He frowned and gazed anxiously at Deormund.

"Ay?"

"Our culture and tradition are so different. We sing to please our gods, who are not yours."

In turn, Deormund laughed. "That is no problem; indeed, quite the opposite. I wish to hear the tales and melodies of a far-off land."

"But do you have an instrument for me? My lyre is lost at sea. At best, it is now in the hands of the Franks."

"He can use mine," Eored offered.

The thegn clapped his hands and a serving maid scurried to him.

"Girl, hasten to Mistress Saewynn; fetch her husband's hearpe."

As she hurried away, he turned to his guest. "Now, *she* is a serving maid, a free woman, not a slave."

Abashed, the skald lowered his gaze and gripped Eored's cloak which was still warming him. "I beg you, Lord, do not associate me with the excesses of my people. Surely, some men disgrace your folk, too?"

Deormund's brow wrinkled and he stroked his beard at the chin. "You speak truly, friend. Before the Norsemen began to raid and plunder our villages, it was our stock from the west or the north who bethought to seize what was not theirs. Except that the men of Wessex and Mercians left Sceapig in peace, whereas now we are open to raids from the sea. Fear not. I see what manner of man you are. Come, I will find you a space to lay your head; we need you to be well-rested for mealtime."

The skald stood, removed Eored's cloak and handed it to him with a grateful smile.

"Nay, keep it! I have another while you have nothing in this world."

Thus, a friendship was born out of a love for music in common.

The skald was strumming Eored's hearpe quietly in a

corner when the menfolk filed into the hall for dinner. Immediately, he became the subject of hushed conversations. When Deormund took his place at the high table, he clapped his hands for silence, in which he announced, "My friends, tonight..." he realised he had not asked the skald his name, "we shall be entertained by a scop, our guest, from a distant land, who will recite a saga from his homeland."

To loud applause and whistles of appreciation, the musician stood and beamed around the hall.

Now was his chance to test his language skills. At first hesitantly, but gaining confidence, he said,

"The tale I am about to sing relates the meeting of Sigurdr with the valkyrie Brynhildr, better known as Sigrdrifa or *driver to victory*."

To most men in the hall, the names meant nothing, but Deormund knew all about the valkyrie and their role in the lives and deaths of the Norsemen. The skald continued, "The first three verses are spoken by Sigrdrifa after she has been awoken by Sigurd and then he sits beside her to ask her name. She takes a horn full of mead..." at this, some of the men laughed and raised their beakers; the scop smiled and went on, "and she gave him a memory draught. B ut let me now begin."

He strummed the hearpe and suddenly, his rich voice with its pleasant timbre filled the hall. The melody and the tone of the strange tongue gripped the audience but, unlike the others, Deormund managed to grasp the sense of the words.

When the bard arrived at the fifth verse, he understood that Sigrdrifa brought Sigurd beer charmed with runes:

> *"Beer I bring thee, tree of battle,*
> *Mingled of strength and mighty fame;*
> *Charms it holds and healing signs,*
> *Spells full good, and gladness-runes."*

Runes interested Deormund. Nowadays, they had become symbols of the past; many people no longer knew their meaning. In his grandsire's day, maybe even before, people understood their meanings and undoubted magic. The new religion of Christ forbade dabbling in runic magic. So, when the scop continued with the sixth verse, he leant forward with particular interest. That verse advised to carve victory runes on the sword hilt:

"Victory runes you must know
If you will have victory,
And carve them on the sword's hilt, some on the grasp
And some on the inlay,
And name Tyr twice."

To the amazement of Eored and Eadlac sitting at either hand, Deormund drew his sword at the table, held the sword by the blade, near the hilt and studied it. He had ceased to follow the bard's tale, which became a background hum to him as he stared at the weapon under his nose. The clapping of hands and a rhythmic beating of cups on tables brought the thegn out of his trance-like state. He called to the scop even as he bowed round the room, milking the applause.

"Scop! Over here, join me at my table for a drink. You will have a thirst."

In reality, he was not at all concerned about the harpist's dry throat: he had only one thing on his mind, but he held his curiosity back as a good host should until the scop had drained his beaker of ale. Drawing his sword for the second time in a matter of minutes, he laid it hilt-first on the table and slid it across to the wide-eyed bard.

His heart beating a little faster than usual, he asked the songster, "Are they not the victory runes of your rhyme?"

Uneasily, the scop traced the t-runes of Tyr with his fingernail, stared up levelly at Deormund and said, "This is the sword of a great chieftain. You must be a mighty warrior!"

It was difficult to determine who among the three men in front of him was laughing the loudest, but he saw nothing amusing in his words.

"These are the magic runes of victory—it is to them the song refers."

His calm, even tone removed the merriment from the faces of the men opposite. Deormund's in particular became grave and concerned. "May I ask, Lord, how you came by this weapon?" His fingers again ran reverentially over the runes.

"I took it from the Norse chieftain I slew."

"Then you are indeed a great warrior, but there is a price to be paid."

Deormund frowned. "What would that be, Scop? Come, do not fear: speak the truth."

The bard was scared. How would this mighty thegn react to his pronouncement? Would the price to be paid be his life, for a start? He gulped and considered the man before him, not daring to formulate the words.

"Well?"

The impatient tone meant he must speak else risk adding timber to the blaze.

"The fact is, Thegn, that this sword is so valuable, I'd say without a price, that the slain chieftain's heir, whoever he is, will come to wrest it back." There, it was said! He gazed anxiously at his host and wondered if, in some way, he could make his words more palatable. He did not expect the reply that came unhesitatingly.

"Let him come! I have waited long and, therefore, I am ready and fear no Viking. Besides, friend skald, I am the bearer

JOHN BROUGHTON

of the victory blade that has already brought me to triumph
over your sea wolves. It will do so again!"

His words were bold and, whilst heartfelt, in that same seat
of his soul he knew that he had the defences prepared,
possessed the sword of victory and, above all, a plan—he would
relish the moment.

TWENTY

SCEAPIG

803 AD

THE LONG, SHRILL BLAST, REPEATED THREE TIMES, ROUSED Deormund from his slumbers. Throwing his clothes on and struggling with the leather thongs of his boots, he fought the pounding of blood in his sleepy head to charge out of the hall and race to the foot of the lookout tower.

"A Viking sail approaching, Lord!"

Without a second's thought, the thegn dashed to the wooden steps and, taking them two at a time, charged to the top. Sure enough, starkly silhouetted against the sparkling sea, dazzling in the early morning sunlight, the unmistakable sleek, square-sailed shape of a Norse longship sliced through the waves towards the coast of Sceapig.

Below in the courtyard, men gathered to squint up the tower against the morning light. The alarm notes had brought them from their beds. Deormund leant over the railings to yell down, "Vikings! To arms! Eadlac, see that they are properly equipped and gather the men behind the gates."

Was today to be the one of reckoning? He unconsciously touched the hilt of his sword—had the chieftain's heir come to reclaim his lord's victory blade? Well, that would prove no easy task! The thegn would relinquish his property but only at a very high price.

"Keep an eye on where they come ashore," he told his lookout. "Shout it down to me."

With that, he bounded down the steps, heedless of risking a fall, in a rush to explain to Eadlac why he would not march alongside his men. On this occasion, Eadlac would face the Vikings as the Sceapig commander.

Gazing unbelievingly into his thegn's eyes, the giant bodyguard struggled to understand. The matter was hard to comprehend because the thegn did not fully take him into his confidences as his plan relied on surprise, not only for the Vikings but also for the islanders.

"All I ask is that you trust me, Eadlac."

"It's not that, Lord, you know I do! But what about the men? When they see that you are not at their head, they'll be dismayed."

"Tell them that I have a plan. All will be clear. Tell them to have faith in Thegn Deormund."

He would say no more. In any case, an alarmed shout came from above.

"They're running straight for Minster Beach!"

"Another blast on that damned horn," the thegn ordered.

The shrill wail brought men scampering into the courtyard. Some had leather jerkins still unlaced while others rammed studded helms on their heads as they rushed to assemble. A glance told Deormund what he needed to know: thanks to his and Sherred the smith's efforts, the island force was well-armed. With all of Wardric's expertise in their minds, the efficiently-trained fyrd would give a good account of itself.

"Take them to the meadow, Eadlac. Heed me well; line up

our men facing west, with the low sun behind their backs so that it strikes the eyes of the Norsemen."

"Ay, Lord."

"I'm away now—remember what to tell them! Let me through the gates!"

Running out, he did not look back, but as he ran, he fumbled for his whistle and blew once: a long note. In moments, Mistig was overtaking him, delighting in the sprint that his master had deemed suitable exercise to start the day. This was all a part of the thegn's plan that he had conceived the year before, but he also wanted to warn Bebbe and Asculf to take immediate refuge in the hall where they would be much safer.

With a heaving chest, he struggled to gasp out the gist of this, only to be contradicted by the old man.

"Nay, I will fight with Eored in the front line."

"Father, you will not! I know you are still as strong as the others, but I charge you with protecting my mother. If we lose the battle, someone will need to take my place to defend our womenfolk and the nunnery. That someone is you! Do not gainsay me!" He turned to his distraught mother and hugged her. "Don't worry! We won't fail; I have a plan." How he hoped that the reality would match his bold words! But he was rewarded with a brave smile from the tearful visage of his mother.

"Ay, all right, Deormund. I'll do as you say."

"Thank you, Father. We'll feast together in victory tonight!"

He left them preparing to hasten to the hall, summoned Mistig, and had him round up the deer. As he approached the meadow, the stag followed him very slowly, harried into obedience by the deerhound. Gratified, Deormund saw his men faithfully lined up with the sun at their backs, its rays flashing off spearheads, javelin points and axe-heads. Viking war cries reached him and, standing still with his herd grazing behind him, he surveyed the scene.

The enemy poured out of the longship and raced across the beach, pausing to allow stragglers to join them. They fanned out and marched menacingly forward in a fearsome line, battering their shields with swords and rhythmically chanting, "Odin! Odin! Odin!" Their formation was just what the thegn had hoped for in his planning.

Now, his training of Mistig paid off. Shouting a command, the hound followed his sweeping hand gesture and began barking, growling and chivvying the dominant male, setting it off on a frenzied headlong plunge. The hinds pursued, while Mistig, obeying his master's shouts and gestures, drove the beasts in a wide, stampeding arc to come around into line with the backs of the advancing Norsemen. Every Viking concentrated on the Saxon force bristling with spears and javelins. Battle-hardened, their shields were ready to parry the first volley of darts, their eyes fixed on the throwers' arms.

The thegn had calculated that each hind in his herd weighed three hundred pounds, the stag even more. The impact would be spectacular. He cut across, taking the shortest way to reach the back of the Norsemen, but had to halt as Mistig drove the stampede, hoofs silent on the soft turf, past him in a chestnut-coloured blur of skittery, muscular stealth. The panicked animals, as Deormund had foreseen, smashed into the backs of the unsuspecting Vikings, sending them sprawling in disarray. In a flurry of limbs, the agile, flailing beasts struggled, like the Norsemen, to extricate themselves. With a roar, Eadlac urged his men into a similar stampede but, differently from the deer, they were equipped with sharp blades. The thegn shouted an order to his hound and gesticulated with his sword, even as he plunged into the seething mass of men. Mistig, obeying his master's command, drove the stag along the meadow, followed by the instinctively compliant hinds.

Deormund's rage increased when he saw that at least five of his deer had died under the flailing axes of the panicked Norsemen. Still, his plan had met with dramatic success.

Free to concentrate on killing, he waded into the fray, hacking, hewing and fending off blows from the dwindling number of enemy survivors. Determined that none of them would outlast the day, he wielded his victory sword with the fury of the renowned berserkers, protected by his steel-plated armour and helm and driven by the wrath of a Saxon defending his homeland. Two-handed, he plunged his blade into the chest of a foe he had downed. Not the slightest trace of mercy crossed his mind as he pulled out the sword, parried a blow from the side and, enraged, twisted to face his next victim.

The entire engagement lasted less than an hour when at last came the time of the final reckoning.

"Lord, this fellow must have been their chieftain," Eadlac called and pointed to a body.

Deormund stepped, swaying with fatigue, towards the corpse. On his bare and bloodied left arm glimmered a gold armlet, worth a small fortune. But it was not the jewel that stopped Deormund in his tracks.

"Ay, he's the leader," he said, with such certainty that his bodyguard stared at him.

"I've seen that face before." The thegn had a flashback to when he had launched a stone so fatally at a disconcertingly similar countenance. "He came for this, his father's sword." He raised the blade. "I swear no Viking fist will ever again close over this hilt; after all, it is marked with victory runes! Did you slay him, Eadlac?"

"Ay, Lord, with a blow to the heart."

Deormund studied the bloodied chest of the young warrior.

"He was a brave man. Wear his armlet with honour, Eadlac."

The bodyguard gasped. Was his thegn giving him the priceless object?

"B-but it is your victory, Thegn."

"Take it, my friend!"

Suddenly, the mighty warrior threw back his head and laughed.

"What?"

"Your plan!" He guffawed again and the men standing nearest to catch every word, including the bellowing smith, echoed his laughter. "You should have seen their faces, Thegn. Nay, not the Vikings'—ours! Trust a deer herder to dream up such an idea. The beasts sent them toppling over like skittles!" He roared with mirth again, accompanied by the merriment of his men, then bent to wriggle the gold armlet off the limp corpse. "It's a good fit," he grinned, "the fellow had muscles to match mine."

"More's the honour then, my friend. Come on, men, take whatever you will! We must burn their bodies and bury our dead. How many?"

"Two. And five hinds, "Eored said, laying a hand on his shoulder. "Do you think we can eat the slain deer this evening?"

"By God, brother, you'd have this rabble devour me out of my hall!" But his grin betrayed his sentiment. In a rapid change of mood, sorrowfully, he shook his head and murmured a quick prayer when he saw that a father was kneeling over his dead son. He sought the words of condolence he needed, but the man anticipated him.

"Nay, Lord, my lad would have wanted this. We have a victory," he choked on the word, "my son saved them!" He pointed up the hill to the abbey and hall. "We all did! Everyone will remember my Wilron as a hero. What more can a father ask for his dead child?" Emotion strangled his words and he hung his head.

"Friend, I will pay for a headstone to be carved with words of glory. I'll beg the Abbess to have him buried in their church-yard. That way, he'll go straight to Heaven."

The creased and weather-beaten face of the fisherman measured the thegn's countenance before mellowing into a gentle smile. "Wilron worshipped you, you know? Thegn Deormund this—Thegn Deormund that! He was right, of course, your words prove that, not to mention your deeds."

The two men embraced, then the thegn issued commands for the clearing of the meadow. It occurred to him that he had forgotten an important detail as his men began the macabre work of piling Viking bodies onto pyres.

"Eadlac, Eored! Gather ten men; we must check that the longship is free of Vikings. Let's see what bounty awaits us."

His eyes swept eastwards across the meadow to where he saw that his beloved deer were grazing contentedly after their madcap escapade. The grey figure of Mistig in the distance made him smile. The islanders owed that dog a considerable debt. There would be venison for him tonight, he promised silently.

They climbed aboard the fine, dragon-prowed vessel, half-expecting resistance, but found not one Norseman on the ship. Their chieftain had led every fighting man ashore. Once other priorities had been dealt with, Deormund would organise the unloading of the barrels. The ale and mead would not go amiss. Nor would the casks of pork fat and pitch, nor the useful range of ropes, cord and twine. Another thought occurred to him. This time, he would not burn the splendid ship. He would arrange for a crew to sail it to Sondwic, a port where he was sure to find a buyer. He would distribute the money obtained among today's fighting men, who would also act as the crew; when they knew of his scheme, they would be eager to sail the craft. The idea of keeping the longship and becoming a sailor did not please him as he much preferred his feet firmly on the island soil.

The rest of the day's commitments kept the thegn busy. Ironically, the islanders used the Vikings' pitch to burn their bodies. After the pyres were reduced to smouldering ashes, he met the grateful Abbess, who proclaimed thanks for the nuns' salvation. The noblewoman was pleased to order a funerary Mass to be sung for the two fallen heroes, while Deormund provided gravediggers for the burials. Repeating his promise of a headstone to the bereft parents of Wilron, he also explained that the victory feast would go ahead.

"Ay, the lad would have wanted that," said his father, "but Lord, forgive me, I'm not in the mood to attend."

"God willing, there will be other celebratory occasions that do not involve killing. All we islanders want is to live our lives in peace."

TWENTY-ONE
SCEAPIG
803- 811 AD

KENT ENJOYED SEVERAL YEARS OF RESPITE FROM THE Viking menace. Every day, Deormund expected the Norsemen to rouse him from his slumber. Thus, he continually assured the islanders' readiness by overseeing arduous combat training sessions twice a month. Also, he ensured the approaches to Minster from the shore were reinforced with ditches and bastions. Despite his alertness, the thegn enjoyed prosperity and contentment.

His first enterprise after the defeat of the raiders was to sell their longship. Many of the crewmen were used to handling smaller craft, so the sailing of the thoroughbred warship came naturally to them. The voyage down the estuary and along the coast to Sondwic proved trouble-free and enjoyable. Deormund half-regretted his intention of selling the ship. Once on shore, his determination hardened, especially after bumping into an old acquaintance, a sheep trader who worked out of Sondwic, conducting business at various places on the coast and up the great river to Lunden. On occasions, he had sought hinds from Deormund in addition to Asculf's ewes, to sell in the city.

"What are you doing in Sondwic, Deormund?" The weathered face broke into a smile, which revealed white lines in the wrinkles around his eyes where the sun never reached. The trader probably never smiled when aboard his boat and about his work, thought Deormund.

"I am Thegn of Sceapig now," the open mouth and raised eyebrows of the merchant gratified the thegn, "I led my men to victory over the Norsemen. Yonder lies the ship we seized; I mean to sell her. You don't know of anyone who might be prepared to pay a fair price?"

The trader's laugh surprised Deormund.

"What?"

"Such a man does not exist in Sondwic, *Thegn* Deormund. Take my advice, if you want a fair price, you will have to auction to the highest bidder."

The trader undertook to spread the word and the bidding was fixed for the afternoon at the forecourt of a waterside tavern. To pass the time, Deormund sat on a wooden bollard not far from where he had moored the ship. To his gratification, he saw several men inspecting the lines of the vessel. One such fellow called to a crewman still aboard. Deormund, watching closely, saw the islander point him out to the inquirer. In moments, the portly figure was casting his ample shadow over the thegn.

"Well met, Thegn, my name is Leonoth. I trade between Kent and Frankia. They tell me your ship is up for sale. Why don't we strike a deal to save you the trouble of an auction?"

Deormund regarded with suspicion the visage with its oily smile and said, "The point of the auction is for me to obtain the best price I can."

The merchant frowned but, aware of the importance of appearances, replaced the scowl with an ingratiating expression. He fumbled inside his purse and withdrew a coin that glinted with gold.

"Let's see," he said, 'you're a thegn, so your wergild will be fourteen and a half ounces of gold, that's six of these beauties —" his plump fingers opened to reveal the splendid piece.

"I know nothing of gold coins; they are a rarity," Deormund interrupted, "I only know my wergild in silver. That would be a fine sum, but of no import, unless you are planning to kill me," he jested.

"Good Lord, nay! But I supposed the ship would be worth at least as much as a nobleman's life."

"Ay, there's a thought, I'll admit."

"This coin is of King Coenwulf. Look, see his name raised around the edge and here, see, the legend DE VICO LVNDO-NIAE—that signifies it was struck in Lunden."

"I know what it means! But it's silver coin that I need. I have to divide the proceeds with my men."

"You can exchange these coins for silver scillingas and probably get more than they're worth." He winked and looked immaculately repulsive to the thegn's distrustful eye.

"Nay, merchant, I will only sell my ship for silver."

The trader's eyes narrowed and he paused for thought. After a few moments, he spoke.

"Well then, I'm prepared to offer you a bag of silver coins weighing sixty pounds. What say you? It is a good price."

"And she's a good craft. I can scarcely bear to part with her," Deormund said. "but well said, your price is a good one. I shall make it the reserve at the auction. Come this afternoon to yon tavern," he pointed, "and if nobody offers more than your sixty pounds, the vessel will be yours."

"Don't be hasty, Thegn. I can fetch that bag of silver in a matter of minutes and you can go happily on your way, with no further bother."

Deormund was beginning to lose his patience. His eyes flashed dangerously. "Heed me well, Leonoth, if you want my ship, you will come to the auction and outbid the others. That's my last word."

The merchant snorted, reminding the thegn of a swine. "Maybe I'll not come to the auction after all."

"That's your choice," Deormund said between clenched teeth and stood up, towering over the rotund trader. "Now, I have important things to do." He strode away in the direction of the tavern, seeking to wash away with ale the bad taste the merchant had left in his mouth.

The auction threw up a brief battle between the plump trader and another wealthy merchant, won, not wholly to Deormund's pleasure, by his earlier acquaintance but at the higher price of eighty pounds of silver. With a smug expression on his face, the winner approached carrying two bulging bags. "Here," he said, thrusting them towards the thegn.

"Not so fast, merchant! Carry them over to the scales for checking."

Leonoth glared at the seller and blustered, "Why? Do you not trust me?"

"I trust no man. Nothing personal, master trader. Eadlac!"

The imposing figure of the bodyguard strode over to join his lord.

"Come with us to the scales, Eadlac. I might need your services."

"Ay, Thegn."

The scales, standing on a wooden bench, were used regularly for this purpose.

The clerk responsible for weighing took them from the trader and made to place the first bag on the platform of the scales.

"Nay, open the bag, shake out the contents," Deormund insisted, "I want to see what it is we're weighing."

The trader protested in vain as out spilt the silver. "They are all coins of Cuthred, struck at Canterbury," the trader blustered. A sheen of sweat on his brow made the thegn so suspicious that he picked up one of the coins and turned it in his hand. Shiny, in mint condition, the coin satisfied his inspection. "Refill the bag and weigh it," he ordered. "Shake out the other bag!"

Leonoth grabbed the clerk's hand. "Stay! What need is there? It is a waste of everyone's time—you've seen the quality of my coins." The voice rose in pitch and the eyes were shifty.

"Ay, that I have, but those in yon bag, not this one. Shake them out, I say!"

Eadlac obliged and his deep voice boomed, "What's this then?" Mixed among the silver coins were roughly-cut grey discs. The bodyguard picked one up with his free hand, while his other seized the merchant by the throat. "Lead, my Lord." He passed the disc to Deormund.

"Try to swindle me, would you? Check his purse, Eadlac. He should have gold coins to compensate for this base metal."

A brief one-sided struggle ended with the trader on his knees and his purse in Eadlac's hand. The scoundrel made no effort to run, knowing it to be futile. His body was not in any condition to make flight an option. Instead, he began to inveigh, "I offered you a fair price! That ship is not worth more than sixty pounds of silver."

Deormund gestured to the clerk. "Gather the silver, replace it in the bag; weigh it and sum the two bags. Leave the base metal on the bench."

After a few minutes, the clerk said, "The full weight of silver is sixty pounds, Thegn."

"Is it now? Be a good fellow and weigh me the discs."

Gathering the grey metal, the clerk placed them on the weighing platform. "Twenty pounds of lead, Lord."

"Eadlac, remove one gold coin from the purse. It is worth much more than twenty pounds of base metal, but the villain must learn his lesson! Oh, and take a silver scilling, too. Give it to our friend; he's earned it." Deormund passed the scilling to the grateful clerk, took the pouch from Eadlac and tossed it on the ground next to the trembling merchant. "Don't forget your lead. The ship is yours now, bought fair and square! Come on, Eadlac, we have business to attend to."

The bodyguard glared at Leonoth. "Count yourself lucky. I don't want to see your face again," he growled. "Ah, Thegn, here's the gold coin."

"Keep it, my friend, it is your share of the spoils."

"Nay, Lord, it is too much."

"It means more silver for our comrades as your part will be already in your hand."

Eadlac blessed the day he had failed to harm this man, who treated him better than a brother.

Deormund decided to share out the silver aboard the ship to avoid attracting undesired attention in the port where, as in every trading station, the worst elements of society tend to lurk. First, he needed to buy passage up the estuary to Sceapig. Silver would serve to convince one of the traders to make the journey later than his usual hour. So it proved. The animal trader he had spoken to on arrival declared himself willing, because he had intended to call at the island to purchase ten ewes from Asculf since he had a request for them from the city.

"I could take three hinds off you, too, Deormund."

"Forget about the silver, the hinds are yours for nothing, in exchange for this passage." They spat on hands and shook on the deal.

The thegn sat on the deck to count out the exact number of

coins. Nobody disturbed him, partly because they knew what he was about and were eager for him to carry out the division. Also, Eadlac stood in front of his lord, his feet apart, planted on the boards and reserved a discouraging glare for anyone coming too close to Deormund. The thegn, remembering his promise, also counted in a share for Wilron and the widow of their other lost comrade. He would spend Wilron's allocation on a head-stone carved in Faversham.

One by one, he called a name and handed the man six scillingas: a small fortune. To each man, he said, "Spend it wisely, friend."

This might be the only time I'll think well of a Viking ship.

The happy faces of his men brightened the voyage back to the island and he prided himself on not having given them the coins in Sondwic, where undoubtedly, they would have dissi-pated at least one scilling on ale. Getting drunken men aboard a ship and then the consequences of the motion on their stom-achs did not bear thinking about. One scilling would buy the family two oxtails at current market prices. Many a Sceapig wife would bless her warrior husband that night and, he, their thegn, had earned himself their unswerving loyalty—although he felt sure he already had it before sharing the prize money.

Transaction completed between Asculf and the trader, Deormund had Mistig drive three hinds aboard the ship. After gazing at the vessel making her way up the estuary as the low evening sun bathed the meadow in cool light and cast long shadows, the thegn strolled cheerfully along the path to the hall.

Little Asculf toddled to meet him inside their home. Deor-mund grabbed him under the arms, raised him high above his head, turned him upside down, righted him and deposited him, giggling, safely on his feet. The little fellow was growing strong under Cyneflaed's watchful eye. As the seasons drifted slowly by, Deormund was pleased to see his boy become a healthy outdoor creature, scampering all over the meadow, roaming into the woods or the more dangerous marshy areas. Whenever he went in those directions, Deormund sent Mistig with him, confident that the hound's intelligence would prevent serious mishaps. By the time he was nine, the boy knew every inch of the island, likely better than even himself, Deormund supposed. Although he was too young to give their names, the youngster knew where the animals and birds lived and how not to startle them. This intimate knowledge of the land would pay great dividends before Asculf's tenth birthday.

TWENTY-TWO
SCEAPIG
811 AD

THE SOUND HE HAD BEEN DREADING ROUSED DEORMUND from his sleep. Four shrill blasts of the lookout's horn had him dressing and cursing his fumbling fingers. Cyneflaed sat up in bed and her frightened expression did nothing for his jangling nerves. Young Asculf stood in the doorway,

"Father, an alarm!"

"I'm not deaf, boy! Out of my way!"

The youngster, stunned, stared at his father's fleeing heels and began to chase after him, ignoring his mother's cries to come back. Man and boy flew up the lookout tower, vaguely aware of the agitated gathering of men they had passed below in the courtyard.

"Lord, four longships approaching. I reckon they're Vikings!"

Deormund pressed a hand to his chest as if to steady his thumping heart and squinted out to the north-east, almost straight into the red disc in the sky. He saw three black squares: sails with their colours robbed by the strength of the sun. The lookout had said *four*; where was the fourth?

"I can see but three ships."

"Over there, Lord," the lookout's finger swung westwards. "For some reason, they've separated."

He was right; the other vessel was heading towards Sceapig more quickly with the breeze behind it.

"Blow one long note, Raedrys, I want the men ready and armed," but even as he spoke, his courage failed him. Four longships—he did the sums—meant a minimum of one hundred and sixty men. They were outnumbered and another deer stampede would be useless against so many warriors. His mind suddenly made up, he ignored Asculf's persistent questioning to stride down the steps to the courtyard.

"Eadlac!" he bellowed.

"Here, Lord!"

"There are four longships approaching. Select our fastest runners to alert the outlying householders. I want them all here fast, within the safety of this compound. Tell them to bring whatever weapons and animals they have. The Vikings are too many for us to risk a direct assault."

In under an hour, the islanders, even those from the farthest part of Harty, arrived inside the enclosure. Deormund addressed the assembled men.

"This is the largest Viking force ever to set foot on Sceapig. We have enjoyed nine summers of peace. That is at an end, but we cannot face them directly. It would be a slaughter."

"What should we do, then, Lord? Await their flaming darts?" It was the youngest brother of the well-diggers from Harty.

Deormund grinned, then his expression darkened.

"Ay, we wait! But we have *our* arrows and can fire down on them. Eored, unlock the storeroom, distribute bows and arrows. Eadlac, send our best archers to man the outer bastions. Five to each one." He smiled at the Harty shepherd. "Thanks to your efforts, we have the water to douse any flames they hail down on us."

"But how long can we hold out in here?" said the same fellow.

"Long enough until we gain victory."

His words were far bolder than the sentiment in his tremulous heart, but they inspired a rousing and heartening cheer. He organised the fetching of straw for temporary beds in the hall before delegating ten archers—too few, but as many as he could spare—to the defence of the abbey towers. Next, he called Cyneflaed to arrange for the cooks to prepare meals for the swollen numbers.

"Father, Father!" Asculf tugged at his tunic.

"What is it, son?" He was too busy for the boy's constant questioning. The lad's inquisitive mind pleased him, but he could not be doing with it right now. "Well?"

"It's Raedrys, he says to come and look."

"Very well." *What are the Vikings up to?*

Standing beside the lookout, Deormund gazed down upon the meadow. A Norseman had hammered a stake into the turf, from which he stretched a rope, the other end attached to an iron bar. With this, he moved in a circle, ploughing that shape into the soft earth.

"They're marking out a perimeter. It is to be a stronghold on our pastures, damn them!"

"Can we not stop them, Lord?"

"Nay, my friend, there is no purpose in that. The fortress is for them to defend themselves from assault at night. We should be ready for their attack, not their *defence*."

Yet he felt uneasy. Raedrys's expression unsettled him, just as had that of the Harty shepherd. He knew that his men trusted him, but it went against their hardy islander nature to sit tight and wait. They wanted to take the attack to the Danes. The thegn knew that was tantamount to suicide and would not allow it. But could he risk having the Vikings shower the hall with flaming arrows? He gazed across at the reed-thatched roof of his home, at eye level from his current position on the watchtower. The reeds appeared as dry as tinder and his heart sank. Was his policy of waiting the best solution? He desperately needed a strategy and the time to think.

The day passed with him watching the meadow excavations with the erection of the Viking stronghold, defended by deep ditches. The entire force had toiled together to complete their work before sunset, after which red and yellow blazes in the darkness revealed their campfires and their flickering light danced over the white linen of the tents.

"I'll let them make the first move," he told his wife, "although I was tempted to send ten archers to set their tents ablaze."

"You don't think they are peaceful traders, then, using Sceapig as a base?"

"Would that they were! It's more likely that they are related to the two chieftains we defeated years ago." He touched his sword hilt. "They've come to wrest the blade of victory from me. But they shall not have it if I have my way."

"Do you have a plan?" Cyneflaed gazed anxiously at her husband, her faith in him as strong as that of any among the islanders.

"Not yet." He could not lie to her. "Try to sleep. I need to think."

The thegn spent a restless night rejecting one tactic after another, each seeming to him worse than the next. It always came back to a simple equation of numbers—the Viking force was too numerous for them. At best, they could pray for steady attrition to sap the foe, but the circumstances also applied to the defenders; as did the possibility of disease spreading in the overcrowded conditions of the respective strongholds. Deormund lay there, fighting off sleep, in the vain hope that he could find a solution. All he achieved was dull thinking owing to weariness.

The next day brought developments. From the watchtower, he delighted in the fleet-footed escape of his stag into the woodlands, but gnashed his teeth and cursed as Viking archers brought down five hinds. This was nothing compared to his rage on seeing clouds of black smoke billowing from what he knew to be the direction of his parents' house. These columns of smoke became a familiar sight throughout the day as the Vikings plundered and torched houses in the lower reaches of the island.

Mid-afternoon, sitting on the lowest steps of the watchtower, Deormund drew his sword and laid it across his knees. His fingernail traced the magic runes incised in the hilt and the blade. At that moment, he came to a decision. Sheathing the weapon, he stood to stride over to the hall.

"Cyneflaed!" His wife came running and behind her, young Asculf. "Wife, I have decided I must go to Faversham to alert Thegn Sibert. It is our only hope of defeating the Norsemen."

"Deormund, it is folly! The island is crawling with Vikings. They will slay you. You cannot go! Say you will not," tears flooded her eyes and her chin trembled, "I beg you!"

"Father, I'll go! I'm little. I know the island better than anyone. They'll not see *me*!" The swagger about the boy made his father smile, but his face hardened at once. "Don't be ridiculous! I won't send my only son where grown men fear to tread. Nay, you will not go, Asculf."

"I will, Father!"

"I forbid it."

Asculf backed away from his father's reach. "If you don't see me go, you won't be able to stop me!" With that, he bounded out through the doorway followed by his mother's wail: "Asculf!"

Deormund dashed out, too, towards the portal and shouted orders, "On no account open the gates! Do not let my son through. Clear?"

The guards looked at each other and shrugged; neither of them had seen the boy and in any case, they would not have opened for him under the circumstances. His father searched the compound, first in the boy's room, then behind the wood-piles, up the watchtower and in the stables. In the end, cursing and beside himself with anxiety, he had to admit that the boy had fulfilled his threat. For a wild moment, he considered chasing out of the enclosure to search for him, but dismissed the idea for several reasons: first, he would draw Viking atten-tion to himself, thereby endangering the boy even more; second, his mother could not bear to lose them both and he was of more use comforting her; lastly, and most important, he had a gut feeling that if anyone could get across the Swale to Sibert, it was Asculf. The boy was astute, he told himself: the way he had slipped out of the enclosure without anyone seeing him proved as much—how the devil had he managed that?

———

YOUNG ASCULF KNEW every inch of the island, beginning with the compound. When he had fled the hall, he had crept along the side of the building, hidden behind a rainwater collection barrel until his father had returned from the gates and re-entered the building, then he had dodged past the stables and pigsties to a place at the palisade near the hen coops. There, he had discovered, maybe eighteen moons ago, a place where a fox had tunnelled into the grounds, lured by the hens. Asculf had widened the hole with his knife and wriggled through unseen just for the fun of doing so on a couple of occasions. Back then, he had reasoned, one never knew when a secret entry or exit might prove useful. Today it did. In moments, he was through, heedless of soiling his clothing, which he brushed down once he was safely under cover.

No thought of real danger occurred to him. His ignorance made him unafraid of Norse blades, only scared of being seen. That was the only peril that bothered him, so his progress from Minster down to the marshes was slow and extremely furtive. Twice, he heard the guttural tongue of the invaders and on both occasions, he vanished into the earth. Only when he reached the marsh did he consider himself safe. Even so, he moved cautiously, taking care not to startle the wildfowl that lived among the sedge and reeds. They must not draw attention to him.

By now, he felt like the greatest man on the island, for he would save his family and the others... unless... "Oh, no," he murmured. A sudden terrible thought had occurred to him. *What if Heorstan has been killed by the Viking?* In that case, he would paddle the ferry himself. *What if the Vikings have destroyed the ferry?* He could not swim across the Swale; the current was too strong and he would drown. *What if I found some wood? I could drift across.*

He shrugged and dismissed his worries. *As Father says, worrying doesn't solve problems. It only makes them worse.* With that idea in his head, he edged through the marshland towards the river. He had collected birds' eggs in this area before; soon, he could hear the sound of the rushing river. Another few paces, and pulling aside some reeds, he found himself staring at an arrowhead levelled at his chest.

"Asculf!" The ferryman didn't shout his name, it was more a loud whisper. "What are you doing here?" Heorstan was squatting down on a raised patch of dry land.

Asculf joined him. He liked the boatman. "I was about to ask you that question, Heorstan."

The boatman chuckled; he had a habit of asking, not answering, questions. "Where's your hound?"

"At the hall, with Father."

"And does your father let you wander the isle with these damned Norsemen around?"

"Nay, he forbade me to leave the enclosure."

"But you are here!"

"Ay. Hark, Heorstan, I'm on my way to get help from Faversham. I need you to take me across the Swale."

"I'll do that, young Master, but we'll go after dark when the current slackens and the Vikings are gone. They were here a while ago, which is why I was hiding before you happened along. We're safe here if we make no noise." His voice was so low that Asculf was unsure of the words but understood the need to keep quiet. In companionable silence, they waited until the daylight faded. Suddenly the ferryman whispered, "Stay here. I'll check that it's all clear." But Asculf clutched his sleeve.

"Nay, Heorstan, I'm smaller and lighter; I'll go."

Before the boatman could argue, the boy slipped away, wraithlike. He scouted around but could see nobody, although voices in the distance told him that there was enemy movement. The Vikings were likely heading back to their stronghold. Next, anxiety gripping him, he hurried to where the ferryboat should be and there it was, inexplicably undamaged, half-hidden among the reeds. Asculf guessed that the Vikings hadn't come across it, or else it would not be in one piece.

Feeling lightheaded with joy, for this meant he could achieve his mission, he returned to Heorstan.

"There's no-one around and the ferry is all right!" he blurted, not attempting to lower his voice.

The boatman, who had been sitting cross-legged on the ground, stood, complained about his aching bones and gathered the bundled cloak that had served as a cushion.

"Let's go then, young Master and hope that they'll let us enter Faversham after dark."

The strong arms of the ferryman shot them across the river in no time. Since the hour was right and with the favourable current, the crossing was effortless. The town gates were still open and they entered unchallenged. There was still just enough twilight to make their way confidently.

The problem arose when they sought to enter Sibert's hall. The guard on the door treated the man and the boy, both grimy from their afternoon in hiding, with suspicion.

"I can't let any riff-raff into my lord's hall."

"Riff-raff? I'll have you know that this is the son of a thegn."

"Oh aye, and I'm King Cuthbert!" the guard sneered.

"Nay, this is Thegn Deormund's son, Asculf, from Sceapig. And he's come on important business."

Now that Heorstan had all of the guard's attention, Asculf dodged unseen behind the guard's legs and disappeared into the hall.

"Oi, where's he gone?" The guard looked around, stepped into the hall and stared into its depths, closely followed by the boatman.

They saw the little fellow talking to a man, who suddenly ruffled his hair and called out, "Thegn Sibert, a word with you!"

"You see," Heorstan told the guard, "Thegn Deormund's son is a plucky little chap."

191

"I knew his father and if the lad is ought like his sire, then he's a firebrand!" The guard grinned.

The young subversive was now gabbling his news to the patient thegn, who looked upon the boy fondly.

"... and there are four of them, Thegn. Four longships and they've been here since yesterday! They've been killing Father's deer and burning all the houses on Sceapig."

"Hold, young fellow! Have they attacked the hall?"

Asculf looked fearful at the thought. "Well, they hadn't when I sneaked away. Minster is the only place they've left alone, so far. Father says they'll attack tomorrow."

The thegn, who had been bending over the boy, straightened and looked at the nobleman next to him.

"You heard that! Four longships! We must summon the fyrd. I'll send messengers at once. They must be here at dawn. We'll sail to Minster beach and march up to the hall. It's better if we unite with Deormund before we destroy the Norsemen."

Asculf thrilled at the thegn's words and understood at once why his father spoke so highly of his former lord.

"We will come with you on the morrow, Lord. May we sleep by the hearth tonight?"

"We?"

"Heorstan is over there," he said, pointing. The ferryman, who had been watching the group of three, bowed under Sibert's gaze, who waved him over.

"Well met, Heorstan. You will sleep by my hearth tonight. In the morning, sail with us and see that this young imp comes to no harm."

"Ay, thank you, Lord, I'll do that," he said, thinking it was easier said than done.

Within minutes, messengers rode out to alert the Kentish thegns and sea captains. Asculf had found one of Thegn Sibert's wolfhounds and was rolling around the floor, wrestling with it. The dog, mock-growling, bounced happily around its new playmate.

"Save some energy for slaying Vikings tomorrow," joked Sibert, getting much nearer the truth than he could ever imagine. Asculf's only weapon lay snugly in his pocket.

TWENTY-THREE
SCEAPIG
811 AD

THEGN SIBERT DECIDED TO REJECT THE IDEA OF SAILING around the coast with his army. Instead, he ordered the captains to lash five boats together athwart the Swale Channel. In so doing, he had effectively created a footbridge across to the south of the island. The advantage of this scheme was that the landing would be unseen by the Vikings, who occupied the meadow situated on the northern side.

Whilst crossing to the north of the channel, Asculf tugged at Sibert's tunic. "Lord, I know the way through the marshes so that we can reach the end of the woodlands without anybody seeing us."

"The boy knows all the by-ways," Heorstan confirmed.

The thegn agreed, instructing his men to keep silent and not to stray off the path their young guide would lead them along. They were repaid for the slowness of their progress by the absence of any alarm, apart from the warbling ones of the occasional grebe they disturbed. At last, they came to the edge of the marsh, where it met the woods.

"Quick, this way! There's a path that leads to the back of the abbey," Asculf hissed to the thegn, who nodded.

The boy and the boatman led the way up the steep trail. When they came out of a bend, they found themselves face to face with a tall Viking, arrow already nocked. Alerted by their footsteps, the archer released the string with a twang. Asculf reacted by shouldering Heorstan, causing him to totter very slightly, enough to take the arrowhead in his shoulder and not the heart. The Viking was raising his horn to blow an alarm call: it was his last act on earth. Asculf had already slotted a stone into the sling in his pocket, stolen along with the missile from his father's room. So, the selfsame pebble that had felled the Norse chieftain years before, now thudded between the eyes of the tall invader. Sibert raced past Asculf, sword drawn and plunged it two-handed down into the chest of the supine warrior.

The thegn kept his voice low. "Well done, lad, I think you killed him, I was only making sure. You stopped him sending the alarm. Let's hope there are no others. How far to the abbey?"

"Not far," came the youngster's laconic answer. He was more worried about the ferryman's wound. He remembered his father saying that there was a nun skilled in healing in the nunnery. They should hurry ahead if Heorstan could manage.

"Only a scratch, boy, don't witter!" the boatman insisted, but Asculf stared at the black-fletched shaft protruding from his shoulder and shook his head.

"Been worse if you hadn't nudged me off balance. I owe you my life." With his good hand, the ferryman clapped the boy on his back. "He's a good 'un, this'un," he said proudly to Thegn Sibert.

"Let's make haste to the healer—she's in the abbey," Asculf urged.

The men standing lookout on the nunnery ramparts could scarcely believe their eyes as more and more Saxons appeared before the entrance. With admirable restraint, they did not cheer or celebrate their relief but ordered the gates to be opened. The thegn entrusted Heorstan to the infirmarian, who clicked her tongue and declared, "All men are stupid from birth." When the boatman found the strength to question her assertion, she replied, "Men spend their lives warring with each other. Look at you, a ferryman who needs his arms to row across the Channel, getting himself impaled by this piece of steel!" She waved the arrowhead under his nose reprovingly.

"You should know, Sister, that I would not have received this wound if I hadn't decided to bring Thegn Sibert and the men of Kent to save your blessed hide."

"Humph!" snorted the infirmarian, not to be persuaded by this wretch who needed her care. Whatever she thought of men, she treated him well and, binding him up, declared that he could now go, as he wanted, to join Thegn Deormund, but "No violent exercise, mind you." The boatman shrugged his uninjured shoulder and agreed.

On arrival at Deormund's hall, Asculf faced the wrath of his father, who raised a hand to chastise him for disobeying orders and running off, only to have it seized by Sibert.

"Your son is a hero!" declared the thegn. "You should thank him and that boatman that we are here to save your skins, deer herder!"

Cyneflaed darted a hostile glance at her husband and snatched Asculf to her bosom. Over her son's head, she said to her spouse, "You should reward our brave little warrior."

"Very well, you are right. My fear for his wellbeing shortened my temper. Here, boy!" Deormund shook three silver coins into his hand and gave them to his son. "Spend them well!"

"I will, Father. I'll buy myself a hound at the next market!"

"Ah, you will, will you? I don't think so," said Sibert. "What will you do with two hounds?"

"Nay, Lord, Mistig is Father's dog. I want my own."

The nobleman chuckled and teased him. "You already have your own! It is that lolloping dog you were rolling around with in my hall. I shall give him to you!"

Asculf broke free from his mother's embrace to launch himself at his benefactor.

"Thank you, thank you, Thegn Sibert!" He hugged the thegn around his thighs.

"Good! But first we have the matter of the Vikings to deal with. It must be midday. I'm surprised they haven't attacked."

The thegn's puzzled frown matched that of Deormund's.

"I've been expecting an assault all morning. Do the enemy know the men of Kent are here?"

Sibert explained the downing of the Viking lookout and how they had arrived unnoticed in almost complete silence.

"So that's where my sling disappeared to, Asculf! Thanks to you, the scout didn't alert the Vikings. So, we have the advantage of surprise. What say you, Sibert, if we send half of this crowd into the abbey? We can await events more comfortably and, if they make no move until dusk, we should attack them by night unawares."

"Meanwhile, I'll dispatch two of my best spies to ensure that *they* do not attack us by surprise," the older thegn said.

"I can be a spy!" Asculf piped.

"Nay! Count yourself lucky I haven't punished you!" his father said. "This time, you'll stay here to protect your mother." He pushed his face into that of Asculf. The fierce expression did not cow the boy.

"Ay, father, I'll slay any Viking that tries to approach her."

"He would, too," said Sibert, full of admiration.

Another voice, deep and mellow, interrupted them. "Let me go, Lord. If I'm challenged, I have the right language and looks."

"By God, a Viking!" Sibert spluttered.

Deormund smiled at his friend's discomfort. "Ay, Torfi the Skald and a firm friend of mine."

"You can't let him go. He'll betray our presence and plans."

Assuming an offended expression, Torfi replied, "I am a man of peace and have no love for those marauders."

Deormund laughed and added bitterly, "Besides, he cannot reveal plans that, even if they exist, are so vague! I say we place our trust in Torfi."

Agreement reached, the skald slipped through the gates, his lyre slung between his wide shoulders and hanging down his back.

Sibert watched him stride out. "I just hope you're right, Deormund."

"We have nothing to lose and everything to gain," replied the younger thegn.

Three hours later, the entry swung open to admit the skald, who strode directly into the hall.

The two thegns took him aside and pressed him for his account.

"It went as I supposed. A guard challenged me at the entrance and I told him I had been in the woods whence he saw me arrive. 'For what purpose?' he asked." The skald treated them to a crooked smile and sniggered, "Luckily, he knew nothing of music. 'Why, to get resin for my lyre.' I brandished the instrument, so he grinned and let me in." The skald paused because he had more important tidings. "I know why they haven't yet attacked."

Deormund leant forward eagerly. "And why is that?"

"They are building a belfry to attack our walls."

198

THE RUNES OF VICTORY

"Impossible!" snorted Sibert, "The man's talking nonsense! If they were building a tower, we'd see it from the ramparts. I've seen no such steeple."

Torfi scowled. "The Vikings are cunning. They know that the path to the hall is steep. They could never push a tower up it. Nay, they will carry the timber, hewn to fit together, like a column of ants carrying crumbs of honey cake. Then, they will assemble it at the edge of the woods and wheel it full of warriors right up to your walls."

"By God! The devils!" Sibert spluttered again. His eyes narrowed. "But how did you get out from their fortress, skald? Is this some trick?"

"You can trust me, Thegn. I waited until the guards changed, then, when the new ones challenged me, 'Where do you think you're going?' I again replied, 'To the woods, to collect resin for my lyre.' They didn't ask me how resin served for a lyre, thank Freya!" He grinned at the relieved faces. "One thing, though, Lord Deormund, they have dug a deep ditch around their stronghold. The entrance to the fortress is in the form of a serpent, but it's the only place to attack without incurring great slaughter."

The two thegns exchanged glances. Deormund spoke first. "Torfi, you have displayed courage—for a scop! Your information is of value. Leave us; we must discuss your tidings."

"One thing is clear, Deormund, we cannot wait here much longer. The Vikings are building their tower. They must never use it."

"Agreed, we should attack with all our men, but you heard what the skald said, that it would be folly to storm the ditch. We must adopt what aid Nature can provide. The enemy thinks we have only our small garrison, so surprise is on our side. We can attack from the cover of the woods, but not in broad daylight. I suggest we wait for dusk.

We need some light, but a volley of flaming arrows into their tents as a first move should illuminate the way. Oh, and we'll have the advantage of advancing with the low sun behind us."

Sibert gazed at the younger man, admiration written on his face. "I always knew you had leadership qualities. I cannot think of a better plan. I will summon the other leaders and explain. Have your archers prepare the arrows for the rain of fire."

A high voice piped, "Lord Sibert, will you truly give me the hound?"

"Asculf, I said so. But there is a condition."

"Anything, Lord."

"Promise you will stay in the hall to protect your mother, as agreed."

"I will. I swear!"

The thegn smiled at the boy. "Oh, there's one more condition..." He revelled in the boy's anguished expression.

"What?"

"That we defeat the Vikings. After all, to make you a gift, I must survive the day!"

Asculf trembled with excitement. "You will win and *will* survive!" It was more a command than a wish. Sibert guffawed, ruffled Asculf's hair and strode off to speak to the leaders of the fyrd.

———

TIME SEEMED to stand still for the waiting Kentish force. Inexorably, the shadows lengthened until, at last, the gates of the hall and the abbey swung open. The men, primed to move in silence, were led down through the woodland by a select group of archers, each equipped with a flintstone and steel striker.

Halting at the edge of the woods, the archers awaited their thegn's command.

Deormund peered across to the Viking fortress and noted with satisfaction the deep shadows cast by the low sun. He calculated the distance from the woodland fringe at two hundred yards, easy enough for his archers to hail down their fire. He gave the order and soon, the oiled rags bound around the shafts caught fire from the sparks.

"Aim, draw, loose!"

The flaming arrows arced into the Norse stronghold, causing an immediate panic. Alarm horns blared while voices shouted orders and curses. Deormund ordered the charge. With the sun low behind them, the Saxons pounded across the turf to the entry of the fortress. The swiftness of the assault and the chaos within engendered by the burning tents meant that the entrance was badly defended. Even so, several men fell to Viking spears, but the sheer weight of Kentish numbers resulted in more Norsemen lying bloodied on the ground, trampled by the surging attackers who broke through immediately.

Once inside the earthworks, the battle was furious and hard-fought. Although outnumbered, four Viking crews were a stern proposition for any adversary. The men of Kent, well-armed and outnumbering the foe, had the advantage of the defenders' disarray. With no question of organised resistance, the Vikings fought every man for himself, often against three adversaries at once. Deormund, desperate to find a Norse chieftain, was as confused as everyone else. With no focal point to attack, because the Viking banners were either burnt or still standing by an undamaged tent, the young thegn selected the tallest and strongest-looking adversary to slay with his victory blade. In this way, he slew four giant warriors before the battle ended in a complete victory for the Saxons.

Thegn Sibert had the honour of dealing the last death blow,

to the glee of his onlooking men formed around like spectators in an arena, howling at every cut inflicted by their leader. Their baying vengeance and primaeval lust for blood sickened Deormund, whose blade had already been sated. Again, the victory runes had triumphed; he raised the sword aloft and vented his tension in a prolonged cry of joy: "*Sceapig!*"

The defeat of these Vikings would, he hoped, keep the isle safe so that he could return to herding his deer and raising his son in peace. With every passing day, young Asculf was proving to be a worthy successor to the Sceapig thegn.

THE END

APPENDIX

As in the frontispiece, an extract from a letter written by the scholar Alcuin from the court of Charlemagne, addressed to the clergy and nobles of Kent in 797 AD

'Imminet uero maximum insulae huic et populo habitanti in ea periculum. Ecce quod nunquam antea auditum fuit, populus paganus solet uastare piratico latrocinio littora nostra.'
Translation: (as on page 41 of the novel)

'A very great danger threatens this island and the people dwelling in it. Behold a thing never before heard of, a pagan people is becoming accustomed to laying waste our shores with piratical robbery.'

For a pleasant brief biography of Alcuin see this link from the British Library.
https://www.bl.uk/people/alcuin-of-york#

Dear reader,

We hope you enjoyed reading *The Runes of Victory*. Please take a moment to leave a review, even if it's a short one. Your opinion is important to us.

Discover more books by John Broughton at https://www.nextchapter.pub/authors/john-broughton

Want to know when one of our books is free or discounted? Join the newsletter at http://eepurl.com/bqqB3H

Best regards,

John Broughton and the Next Chapter Team

AN APPEAL TO READERS: PLEASE HELP ME OUT—

I sincerely hope you enjoyed *The Runes of Victory*.

First and foremost, I'm always looking to grow and improve as a writer. It is reassuring to hear what works, as well as to receive constructive feedback on what can be improved. Second, starting out as an unknown author is exceedingly difficult, and Amazon reviews go a long way toward making the journey out of anonymity possible. Please take a few minutes to write an honest review. I would greatly appreciate it.

Best regards,

John Broughton

ABOUT THE AUTHOR

 John Broughton was born in Cleethorpes Lincolnshire UK in 1948: just one of many post-war babies. After attending grammar school and studying to the sound of Bob Dylan, he went to Nottingham University and studied Medieval and Modern History (Archaeology subsidiary). The subsidiary course led to one of his greatest academic achievements: tipping the soil content of a wheelbarrow from the summit of a spoil heap on an old lady hobbling past the dig. He did many different jobs while living in Radcliffe-on-Trent, Leamington, Glossop, the Scilly Isles, Puglia and Calabria. They include teaching English and History, managing a Day Care Centre, being a Director of a Trade Institute and teaching university students English. He even tried being a fisherman and a flower picker when he was on St. Agnes island, Scilly.

He has lived in Calabria since 1992 where he settled into a long-term job at the University of Calabria teaching English. No doubt his lovely Calabrian wife Maria stopped him being restless. His two kids are grown up now, but he wrote books for them when they were little. Hamish Hamilton and then Thomas Nelson published six of these in England in the 1980s.

They are now out of print. He's a granddad and, happily, the parents gratifyingly named his grandson Dylan. He decided to take up writing again late in his career. When teaching and working as a translator, you don't really have time for writing. As soon as he stopped the translation work, he resumed writing in 2014. The fruit of that decision was his first historical novel, *The Purple Thread* followed by *Wyrd of the Wolf*. Both are set in his favourite Anglo-Saxon period. His third and fourth novels, a two-book set, are *Saints and Sinners* and its sequel *Mixed Blessings* set on the cusp of the eighth century in Mercia and Lindsey. A fifth *Sward and Sword* is about the great Earl Godwine. Creativia Publishing has released *Perfecta Saxonia* and *Ulf's Tale* about King Aethelstan and King Cnut's empire respectively. In May 2019, they published *In the Name of the Mother*, a sequel to *Wyrd of the Wolf*. Creativia/Next Chapter also published *Angenga*, a time-travel novel linking the ninth century to the twenty-first. This novel inspired John Broughton's next venture, a series of seven novels about psychic investigator Jake Conley, whose retrocognition takes him back to Anglo-Saxon times. In another departure, he published a fantasy novel, *Whirligig*.

In all, he has twenty-three novels published, which can be seen with relative information at the author's website: www.saxonquill.com